BLOOD SIGHT

Lee Kershaw looked toward the darkened canyon. A breeze sprang up. Metal clicked against rock high on the moonlighted slopes overlooking the labyrinth. Lee hit the ground a fraction of a second before the Sharps bellowed and sent an explosive bullet whispering right over where Lee had been standing. The bullet blew itself up against the rocks fifty yards beyond Lee. The breed sonofabitch was shooting by instinct. No living man could have seen Lee in those shadows—no living man but Queho, that is. . . .

Renegade's Trail

Gordon D. Shirreffs

FAWCETT GOLD MEDAL • NEW YORK

A Fawcett Gold Medal Book
Published by Ballantine Books
Copyright © 1974 by Fawcett Publications, Inc.

ISBN 0-449-13141-6

Manufactured in the United States of America

First Fawcett Gold Medal Edition: April 1974
First Ballantine Books Edition: August 1988

AUTHOR'S NOTE

There was a halfbreed named Queho in the wild country where Arizona, California, and Nevada come together. In the early 1900s, he ran amok, but not wildly. He haunted the canyons and barrens, and unseen he picked off his victims with a rifle or perhaps with a knife. Legend has it that he killed twenty-three victims—sheepherders, travelers, prospectors, and lawmen. The number of victims included men, women, and children. Some say he killed no more than twelve people, but a dozen *or* twenty-three equally established him as a homicidal maniac. His first victim was murdered in 1910; his last known victim was a woman murdered in 1919. During the intervening years, some of the best manhunters and trackers in that area, white men and Indians both, found traces of Queho, but they never saw their quarry. Two prospectors were found murdered and mutilated after the death of the woman, but it has never been established that Queho was the murderer, although it is quite likely that he was. The posse that hunted Queho after this double murder did not find him, but they did find the skeletons of two unidentified men who had been murdered in that same area five years past. Three thousand dollars in rewards was offered for Queho's apprehension, but it was never collected.

Eleven years after the murder of the woman and the two prospectors, in the year 1930, Queho was seen in Las Vegas. He bought a can of peaches in a grocery store, paid for it, and departed from the store. He walked on Fremont

Street in broad daylight and then walked into oblivion and local history. He was never seen alive again, and if he committed any other murders after that, it has never been established that he did.

In 1940, two prospectors five miles upriver from El Dorado Canyon spotted a small cave near the base of a hundred-foot sheer cliff. The area is of volcanic origin, and caves are many. What drew the attention of the two prospectors was that the cave mouth was closed with a carefully laid rock wall. They broke down the wall and found the mummified body of Queho. Within the cave the prospectors found a Winchester rifle and a Hopkins and Allen shotgun, as well as a bow and arrows. There were empty and loaded cartridge cases, primers, powder and bullets, tobacco cans, various reloading tools and other tools, and a watchman's badge Number 896. The watchman had been murdered by Queho at the Gold Bug mill thirty years earlier.

The mummified remains of Queho were and may still be exhibited in the Las Vegas Elks Helldorado Village, along with his goods and chattels.

For my book *Renegade's Trail*, I borrowed only the name of Queho and the hideout cave in which he lived. The rest is fiction.

Gordon D. Shirreffs

ONE

IT WAS NEARING the Time of Little Eagles in Arizona Territory. A cold early spring wind swept fine gravel from the barren floor of the Hualapai Valley and bitter alkali dust from the dry Red Lake bed hard against the taut faces of the two men who stood at the heads of their tired horses looking to the north toward the distant and unseen Colorado River Canyon.

Lee Kershaw turned at last from the searching wind and stepped behind his dun horse to feel for the makings within his sheepskin jacket. "He's either headed for the Crossing or he's damned sure to be hiding out with the Hualapais," he suggested.

Queho turned to look at Lee. His strange, light-colored eyes, so startling in contrast with his dark face and thick, dark lips, studied the white man. "No risk the Crossing," he said quietly. "Hualapais all gone. You white men took them from home here, maybe eight years ago, to La Paz on Colorado. Many died there. Hualapais all gone, Kershaw. You knew that."

Lee lighted the cigarette within the sheltering cup of a big hand and then placed it between the thick lips of the breed tracker. He began to shape one for himself. He nodded. "I had forgotten," he said.

"I did not."

Lee nodded again. "I had nothing to do with it, Queho."

"But you're white," argued Queho.

Lee lighted the cigarette. "Don't start that all over

3

again," he quietly warned. "We came north to find Ahvote. Remember?"

Queho looked south. "Willow Grove Spring," he said.

"That's thirty miles southeast of here! Why the hell would he head south right back into the faces of the men following him?"

Queho took his cigarette from his mouth and looked at it as though he had never seen one quite like it before. "Maybe the woman be there now," he quietly suggested.

Kershaw looked quickly at him. "Mrs. Felding?"

Queho nodded. "Colonel Felding leave Prescott for Fort Mohave Reservation on inspection trip. Wife go along, eh?"

Lee nodded. He grinned. "He damned well wouldn't leave her back at Prescott with all the male wolves snuffling around her broad rump."

"He stay at Fort Mohave awhile, then take steamer to Yuma."

Lee looked thoughtfully to the southeast. He was tired, although he'd never admit it to the breed. When he moved in the saddle, the knife wound in his back, which had healed slowly because of infection, ached dully, and there was hardly any position he could take to ease the pain. He had been hurriedly drafted from a damned good poker game to start out after Ahvote, who had broken loose from the *juzgado* and killed a guard in the process. Ahvote was good at killing, a real professional by now.

"Ahvote want woman," added the breed.

"He's loco!" snapped Lee. "There'll be at least ten troopers with Felding and his wife."

"Ahvote want woman. Ahvote *get* woman."

Lee studied the scarred dark face of Queho. The man had an uncanny ability to forecast coming events.

"No sense to go on to river," said Queho.

"That's the way he went two months ago."

"Mean nothing."

Lee leaned against the dun. His shoulder was throbbing.

4

It wouldn't take much argument from the tracker at that to get Lee to turn back. Two things prevented him—to show weakness in front of Queho and to admit that Queho was right in that Ahvote *had* gone south, for Lee's pride would not let him admit that Queho was a better tracker than himself.

Queho knelt and passed a dark and powerful hand down the left rear leg of his sorrel. "Horse go a little lame soon," he said.

"Goddamn it! Anything else?" snapped Lee.

Queho stood up. "You know I'm right, Kershaw," he said quietly. "Besides, Queho responsible for you, Kershaw. You know that too."

"That's the Paiute in you talking now," sneered Kershaw.

Queho shook his head. "Mohave Apache," he corrected. "Ahvote Chemehuevis Paiute. *Not* Queho!"

Kershaw began to unstrap a saddlebag. "So, the Mohave Apache in you saved my life two months ago when Ahvote stuck a knife in my back and was ready to finish the job when you caught up with him."

He turned to look at the scarred face of the breed. Ahvote's knife had cut across Queho's broad nose and just under his left eye to score down to the bone clear to the point of the chin, missing the jugular only by inches. "What about the white man in *you?*" he added. "Are you your brother's keeper, Queho? God knows himself that you have nothing to owe to any white man."

Queho studied the lean, brown face of Lee Kershaw, thin from the loss of blood when Ahvote's knife-tip had sought his life source. "Maybe you forgot nigger blood too, eh, Kershaw?" he queried.

Lee took out the brandy bottle. He pulled the cork out with his teeth and drank deeply and again, until he felt the life-giving jolt of the brandy deep in his lean guts. He wiped his mouth with the back of a hand and held out the bottle to the breed. Queho shook his head. "Not now, Kershaw. One of us got to stay sober."

"Who's going to get drunk?" demanded Lee.

Queho shrugged. "Maybe you. You got three whole bottles to yourself. Go ahead. Kill the pain. Queho take care of you."

"Up your ass!" snapped Lee. He drank again. The breed was right. Lee would never make it to Willow Grove Spring without killing the pain.

TWO

THE CAMP AT Willow Grove Spring slept in the cold and windy darkness before the coming of the dawn. Now and again the wind would sweep an invisible paw across the wide, thick bed of ashes that covered the still smoldering fire. When it did so, the red eyes of the embers would light up fitfully, and in the dim, uncertain light could be seen the forms of the troopers huddled under their blankets, furred by ashes, with their feet toward the fire and their heads buried from sight under the blankets. The horses and mules stood with their rumps to the keen wind and with their heads hanging low, picketed in a line among the thin skein of willows that curved around the shallow pool of water seeping from the rock formation above and behind the camp. When the fire flared up, the dim light would reflect itself from the dusty windows of the lone dougherty wagon. All that moved about the camp were the wind-thrashed willows; the flapping sides of the single A-tent that stood like a geometrically shaped ghost beyond the campfire and the dougherty wagon, and the thin wraith of white smoke that drifted downwind from the periodically aroused fire.

Ahvote came through the cold and windy darkness as silently as the drifting smoke. He stood in the darkness beside a tip-tilted slab of rock that thrust itself up from a rise above the spring. Nothing moved about Ahvote except for the slow rise and fall of his deep chest and his restless eyes as he scanned the camp. Earlier, there had been only one sentry, but now he was not in sight. But now, as the fire flared up higher in a strong gust of wind, the light reflected from something that protruded from the half-open door on the lee side of the dougherty wagon. It was a booted foot with a polished spur strapped to it—it was the spur that had caught the firelight. Even as Ahvote watched, the foot moved and then turned over, to be joined by the other foot as the sentry shifted to get into a more comfortable position out of the cold pre-dawn wind.

Ahvote vanished noiselessly into the darkness as the sentry suddenly sat up sleepily within the doorway of the wagon to glance toward the blanket-covered form of Sergeant Elias Bentinck, in charge of the agent's escort to Fort Mohave. The sentry yawned prodigiously, mentally debating whether or not he could get a little more shut-eye before dawn. He never heard the opening and closing of the door on the windward side of the vehicle. He threw back his head to yawn and stretch, just in time for the razor edge of the butcher knife to rip open his taut throat-muscles from ear to ear. The body was pulled back into the dougherty. The door was closed. The other door silently opened and then was closed. The camp seemed just as it had been before the killing. The only difference now was the soft sound of blood dripping through a crack in the floor of the dougherty.

The blood-wet knife sliced through the back of the tent, and Ahvote stepped inside. An Argand lamp with the wick turned down as low as possible stood on a camp table. A cot stood on each side of the tent. A man snored softly in one of them; a woman breathed heavily in the other. Ahvote gathered together some of the woman's clothing and gear. Silently he left the tent and as silently returned. He stood for a time looking down at the red face and fat throat of "Kentucky Colonel" Will Felding, special inspecting agent for the Indian Bureau. Ahvote's strong hand tightened spasmodically about the haft of his knife as he looked at the red face of the man who had been the cause of sending him to prison in Prescott. He looked toward the huddled form of the woman. It had really been her who had been the cause of it, on second thought. She who had lied and *lied* about Ahvote to the fat white man and anyone else who would listen to her! To kill the fat white man would be sweet indeed, but revenge would be better served by stealing the fat one's woman and then laughing at him, from many miles of distance between them of course, as he laid the white woman again and again until she would beg for mercy.

The familiar spoor of the woman rose to meet his flared nostrils—the definable combination scent of female sweat, face powder, and expensive perfume. He had known that scent at Prescott.

Once the fat man rolled over and let a thick arm drop a hamlike hand onto the canvas groundcloth of the tent, but he had turned toward the windbellied wall of the tent instead of toward the side of the tent where his wife should have been sleeping. Had he done so and opened his eyes he would have seen the twisted blankets that now trailed down to the tent floor, and the emptiness of the cot itself.

Once, as the first gray tint of the false dawn washed against the eastern sky, a mule snorted in warning at the Indian smell, but after that, the camp returned to its normal routine of thrashing willows, bellying tent-canvas, and wind-drifting smoke.

THREE

COLONEL FELDING DISMOUNTED awkwardly from his tired bay and reached for his cased field glasses hanging from the saddle. The insides of his fat thighs were chafed raw and wet from hours in the saddle, but he could show no agony on his face in front of the hard-assed escort troopers, who had dismounted from their worn-out mounts and stood down the slope watching him and Sergeant Elias Bentinck. It had been Bentinck who had called Felding's attention to the movement on the side of the mountain to the north. Felding's thick fingers fumbled clumsily with the focusing screw of the field glasses. His breathing was harsh and heavy. Will Felding was a man whose blood pressure was dangerously high. He peered through the powerful glasses. "By God, Bentinck," he said in a strangled tone. "It's them all right!" He handed the glasses to the soldier. "By God," he added brokenly, "we'll never catch up with them now!"

Bentinck focused the glasses. First the pale face of Mildred Felding came into view. Her long blond hair (peroxided secretly at regular intervals, so as not to show the dark roots) hung down alongside her rather round face and over her magnificent bosom (all of it real), held up by the very latest type of support imported from Kansas City. Her shoulders were slumped, and she sat her saddle with her hands resting on the pommel. Bentinck shifted the glasses and picked up the dark face of Ahvote. The man stood at the head of the mule he had been riding, looking down toward the pursuit party. He did not seem much concerned. Why should he feel concerned? The troopers' stubby .45/70 carbines could never reach him at that range, at least with any accuracy, and by the time the troopers reached the foot of the precipitous trail, it would be long dark and he would be long gone beyond the mountain.

"Well?" Felding asked Bentinck.

The trail was narrow and treacherous, hardly a yard wide, with a two-hundred-foot sheer wall above it and a two-hundred-foot sheer wall below it. The foot of the trail was at least two miles away from the pursuit party. The trail seemed to turn into the mountain itself two-hundred yards beyond where the Paiute stood looking down at them. There was about half an hour of daylight left.

"Damn you!" snapped Felding.

Bentinck lowered the glasses. "The only thing we can do, sir, is to keep pushing him."

"The horses are worn out!"

"So are the men, sir."

"That's my wife up there!"

"Listen to *him*," murmured Trooper Nolan to Trooper Cassidy.

"Well, he can't call her a whore in front of us," said Cassidy wisely.

"Shut up there!" snapped Corporal Frantz.

"Ye *know* we're right, Corporal darlin'," murmured Cassidy.

"It was she who led that poor bastard on up there whin she was back at Whipple Barracks," added Nolan. "Wigglin' that fat rump of hers in front av any would-be stud."

"Like you," suggested Trooper Schmidt. "The voman iss a bitch!"

Frantz opened and closed his mouth. They were right. Besides, Felding could not hear them, and Bentinck would have agreed with them if he was not wearing three stripes.

"What to do!" cried Felding in agony. "She's so lovely! So sweet! So young! So helpless!"

Cassidy rolled his eyes upward. "Like a she-wolf in heat," he said.

Felding reached for Bentinck's booted carbine. "I'll kill her myself rather than let him ravish her!"

"We can't reach up there with a carbine, sir," reminded Bentinck.

"There are two men coming up the trail, Sergeant Bentinck!" called out Frantz.

Bentinck turned and raised the glasses. The lead rider was a cigar-smoking white man, a lean lath of a man whose reddish beard fluttered in the cold wind. The second man was a breed. "It's Lee Kershaw, sir," said Bentinck over his shoulder, "and that stinkin' breed Queho."

"Thank God!" cried Felding. "Kershaw will know what to do!"

Bentinck lowered the glasses. "Shit," he said under his breath.

Lee Kershaw waved a casual hand at the troopers (almost *too* casual, thought Corporal Frantz) and reined in his tired dun beside Felding and Bentinck. Queho dismounted and took the reins of Kershaw's dun as Lee dismounted. Lee eased his crotch and shifted his cigar from one side of his mouth to the other. "What's up?" he asked. Bentinck wordlessly handed him the glasses and pointed toward the mountainside. Already the hollows were inked in with shadows as the cold-looking sun sank westward. It didn't take Bentinck long to clue Kershaw in about what had happened at Willow Grove Spring.

Lee lowered the glasses and whistled softly. He looked back at Queho. "You were right," he said.

Felding caught Lee's fruity breath. "You've been drinking on duty!" he accused.

Lee nodded. "Keeps off the chill of the day," he agreed.

"What can we do now, Kershaw?" asked Felding.

Kershaw shrugged. *"Nada,"* he said.

Felding glanced toward the Sharps rifle in the long, embossed saddle-scabbard on Lee's dun. "Maybe you can reach him with the Sharps, Kershaw? You know that rifle better than I ever did. Will you try?"

"He's been drinking," put in Bentinck. "I'll try, sir."

Lee shifted his cigar. "*Never* volunteer," he said quietly.

"Maybe five hundred yards," said Bentinck.

"Closer to six hundred and fifty," corrected Lee. "No soldier-trained shot can make a hit on Ahvote at that range in this light, and uphill at that."

"Seven hundred yards," said Queho. It was the first time he had spoken. No one paid any attention to him. No one but Lee, that is.

"Well?" asked Felding. "By the time you get around to it, Kershaw, the Paiute will be gone."

"It's a wonder he's not gone now," said Lee drily. He raised the glasses again. He picked up the pale, frightened face of the woman. *Bitch,* he thought.

"You know there's no other rifle like that in this Territory," reminded Felding. "I won every damned match I ever entered with it before you came along and beat me at poker for it."

"Only two cases primed and loaded, Kershaw," reminded Queho. "No time to load more now."

"You let him call you that?" asked Bentinck. "He doesn't call you mister?"

Lee shrugged. "He's my friend. He saved my life." He jerked a thumb at the breed. "Get the Sharps," he added. He spoke out of the side of his mouth: "At least I *think* he's my friend."

"He might very well be the only one you've got," said Bentinck.

Lee eyed the truculent noncom. "That gives me some grace," he murmured.

Felding stamped back and forth in his impatience. He was tired. Ever since he had married Mildred two years past and had taken her on his inspection trips throughout the Southwest, he had been trying to act the part of a man twenty-five years younger than he was. The act was wearing him out, although he'd be the last to admit it publicly.

"Better use the Vollmer," advised Lee.

Queho nodded. He swiftly removed the vernier-tang sight from its mount and then quickly fitted the fine ten-power scope to the top of the long rifle. The scope was precision-made of the finest German glass by Vollmer of Jena, who had no peer in the business. It had cost Felding a small fortune in Denver. Queho lowered the breechblock and used the bullet-starter to seat the paper-patched 370-grain bullet in the rifling just ahead of the chamber.

"He'll be gone by the time the breed gets it loaded!" said Bentinck.

"Shut up," said Lee. "There's still time."

Queho withdrew the bullet-starter and slid the long brass cartridge loaded with 70 grains of powder into the chamber. He closed the breech and full-cocked the eleven-pound rifle. He held it out toward Lee. Lee shook his head. "You're on, Queho," he said quietly. "I can't risk a shot with this brandy in me."

"You're loco!" said Bentinck. "That breed can't shoot!"

"Watch him," said Lee. He turned and let Queho rest the long barrel on his shoulder. He took the cigar from his mouth, so that the smoke would not blow across the end of the telescope.

"Drunk or sober, you're the best shot here!" cried Felding to Lee.

"By the time we get through arguing," said Lee out of the side of his mouth, "Ahvote will be out of sight. Shoot, Queho, and be damned to them!"

Queho drew back on the rear trigger. The front trigger clicked faintly as it was set. Queho placed the tip of his finger against the front trigger and drew in a deep breath as he sighted. He let out half of it. For a few seconds the breed was absolutely motionless; then his fingertip almost imperceptibly tightened.

"Don't hit him in the head," said Felding suddenly. "I want his skull for a tobacco jar!"

Lee felt Queho move at Felding's callous remark a fraction of a second before the Sharps crashed out flame and smoke and sent a bellowing echo racing along the ground. An acrid cloud of smoke blew back against Lee's face.

"Goddamn you, breed!" yelled Bentinck as he looked through the field glasses. "You damned near hit Mrs. Felding! The Paiute is moving along the trail! Give me that rifle!" He handed the glasses to Felding and ripped the rifle from the hands of the breed, backhanding Queho with his free hand as he did so. Queho reeled back against Lee, blood leaking from the side of his mouth. "I'll get him, sir!" cried Bentinck as he snapped down the breechblock. Lee caught the empty cartridge-case before it could damage itself on the hard ground. As he came upward again, his right hand closed about the cartridge to form a hard fist, which hit Bentinck on the point of the jaw to drive him hard-assed onto the ground, while with his left hand, Lee ripped the rifle from the soldier's hand. He swung and handed the rifle to Queho. "Reload!" He snatched the field glasses from Felding and focussed them on the mountain trail, while Queho swiftly loaded the smoking Sharps with a packed bullet and the last primed and loaded case.

Ahvote was leading his mule and the woman's horse along the trail. Queho handed the rifle to Lee. He turned to let Lee rest the Sharps on his broad shoulder. With no trace of the good brandy evident, Lee sighted on Ahvote. He set the front trigger and tightened his finger on it. For a few seconds he was as motionless as Queho had been; then the Sharps crashed.

The troopers cheered, not so much because the woman had been saved as for the fantastic skill of Lee Kershaw. The big slug had hit Ahvote almost at the instant of his turning off the trail and out of sight. The Paiute had fallen, arms and legs stiffly outthrust, to pinwheel down into the shadows at the foot of the two-hundred-foot drop below the trail.

The shot echo died; the smoke drifted off.

"Thank God," breathed Felding. "Bentinck, go up there and get my wife."

Bentinck slowly wiped the blood from the side of his mouth. His hard green eyes never left Lee Kershaw. He said nothing, but the warning was evident in his eyes. He would not forget.

"There just might be a killin' between those two some day," suggested Trooper Nolan as he watched Bentinck ride with two men toward the foot of the trail. "That is, if Kershaw hangs around long enough."

"Aye," agreed Cassidy. "Ten dollars on Bentinck," he added.

"Ye're on," agreed Nolan, "but I think I shud give ye odds, Tim."

Felding looked at Corporal Frantz. "Get an oat sack for the breed here, Frantz," he ordered. "Queho, you go and get Ahvote's head for me."

Queho did not move. His dark face was enigmatic, but his strange, light-colored eyes swiveled to look toward the shadowed base of the mountain.

Frantz brought the oat sack to the breed but Queho would not take it. The noncom looked at Felding and shrugged.

"Take the sack, Queho," ordered Felding.

Lee bit off the end of a fresh cigar and cupped a lighted match about the tip of it. "He won't go near the newly dead, Felding," he said around the cigar. "At least not one he was instrumental in killing."

"That's Indian superstition!" said Felding.

Lee nodded as he fanned out the match. "Yup," he agreed. "It surely is. Besides, it's real enough to him."

"But he's only a breed! What the hell difference would it make to him?"

Lee shrugged. "Sometimes he thinks like a white man and sometimes he thinks like an Indian."

"You forgot nigger," said Corporal Frantz.

The sun was gone, and the wind had turned colder.

Lee ejected the cartridge case from the fine Sharps. He placed a wet patch in the chamber and pushed it through with a wooden wiping stick.

"I can order him to go," said Felding at last.

Lee shook his head. "You've got no authority over him," he said.

"He's a government scout, isn't he?"

Lee shook his head again as he started a second patch through the rifling. "Only when they needed him and they paid him by the day. They never honored him by taking him on the payroll. He's done his job. He found Ahvote, after you did, of course, but he knew Ahvote had come back south, which is more than I did."

"How did he know?" suddenly asked Felding.

Lee slid the Sharps into its long saddle-scabbard. "Beats the hell out of me," he replied. He looked sideways at Felding. "Maybe it's the Mohave Apache in him," he slyly suggested.

Felding flushed. He thrust out a thick finger toward the face of the breed. "You get your ass over there and get that goddamned head, breed, or you'll never get another job from the government!"

"Caesar has spoken," drily commented Lee. He swung up into his saddle. "Come on, Queho. Let's find some water. I'm hungry."

Queho turned toward his sorrel.

"I'm warning you!" roared Felding.

"He's coming with me," said Lee.

"To Prescott?" asked Felding.

Lee shook his head. "I had a bellyful of Prescott. I'm heading out of this country."

"Where to?"

Lee shrugged. "Fort Mohave, then maybe down the river to Yuma. After that? *¿Quien sabe?* Maybe the sun of Sonora will help heal this damned shoulder of mine."

"And he's going with you?"

"If he wants to," replied Lee.

Queho mounted the sorrel. "I go," he said simply.

"Wait," said Felding. He came closer to Lee and looked up into the bearded face shadowed beneath the hatbrim. For a moment Lee almost thought the agent was going to thank him for killing Ahvote and saving Milly Felding's life. "I want that rifle back, Kershaw," said Felding. "You know, like a trophy. After all, it did save my wife's life. Of course, you did kill Ahvote, but you'd never have made it without my rifle. I want it back, Kershaw."

"Like another trophy? Like Ahvote's skull for a tobacco jar?" Lee drew in on the cigar, and the flaring of the tip lighted his hard, gray eyes as they studied the face of the agent.

Felding nodded eagerly without catching Lee's point. "A pair of great conversation pieces for a cosy corner in the fine house I'll build some day for Milly and myself, Kershaw. Now, I'm willing to pay you double of what you think it's worth."

Lee touched the dun with his heels and kneed the horse away from the agent. He rode off down the slope followed by the breed.

"God damn you, Kershaw!" roared Felding. "Who the hell do you think you are?"

Lee looked back over his shoulder. "Why, *I'm* Lee Kershaw, *Colonel*. Now, who the hell do you think *you* are?"

Lee and Queho disappeared into the shadows far down the slope. The last sound the men on the rim of the slope heard was the crashing of an empty brandy bottle on the rocky ground; then it was quiet again, except for the dry, cold voice of the wind.

FOUR

A COLD, SEARCHING April wind swept across the barren country beyond Fort Mohave. It drove grit and gravel like buckshot against the post buildings and pitted the dusty window-glass. It rattled the halyards of the tall, warped flagpole and shaped the snapping garrison flag into what seemed like a sheet of corrugated iron painted in red, white, and blue. The Colorado River at the western edge of the post was being driven in hard-looking white-topped waves against the California shore. The wind tugged at the steamer *Mohave,* which was moored to the post's sagging wharf. Chunk firewood cut and piled by reservation Mohave Apache and Chemehuevis at the foot of the wharf was being carried aboard the *Mohave* for her return run downriver the next day. Metal clanged against metal as the engineers repaired the slow-speed, cross-compound engine to ready it for the dawn departure-time for Ehrenburg, where it would pick up ore from the dying placer mines of La Paz and Ehrenburg, as well as passengers from Wickenburg who waited at Ehrenburg for the down steamer.

The sun was slanting down over the California mountains when Lee Kershaw and Queho boarded the *Mohave* with most of their gear, destination Yuma. While Queho stowed away the luggage in the tiny double-bunked cabin reserved for Lee, Lee went out on deck. He bit the end from a long nine and lighted it. He raised his gray eyes over the end of the cigar to look across the dusty parade ground to where Mildred Felding and her husband were walking toward the wharf, followed by half a dozen troopers carrying their luggage and whose eyes were fixed on that fascinating rump action of Milly Felding. They weren't alone in their observations. The eyes of every other man on the post were looking around corners, from within doorways, or through dusty, gravel-pitted windows at that rump.

"I get saddles and other gear now," said Queho from behind Lee. "Where I sleep?"

"There are two bunks in there," replied Lee.

"You know I no can stay in there."

"You can as far as I'm concerned."

"But not him," said Queho. He jerked his head toward Captain Jack Mellen, who was descending the ladder from the pilothouse. "No Indian, no breed, sleep in cabins."

"I paid first-class passage for two," said Lee.

"Kershaw know better."

The breed was right, thought Lee.

"Someday I get you trouble—much trouble," said Queho.

Mellen came toward Lee. "Glad to have you abroad, Lee. Poker tonight?"

"Glad to be aboard, Jack. I might try a hand or two. You don't really need me though. Will Felding will stay up all night with you if you mention a game."

Mellen nodded. "Some say his wife is better at the game than he is," he observed as he watched her approaching the end of the wharf.

"She's better at a *lot* of games than he is," added Lee.

"It's a wonder he isn't wise to it—everyone else seems to be."

"I said she was better at playing games than he was," reminded Lee.

Milly was being helped onto the gangplank, displaying a high-buttoned patent-leather shoe rather tightly fastened about a too plump calf. As she raised her head, she boldly looked up into the eyes of Lee Kershaw. Jack Mellen did not miss the look. "They'll be in the next cabin to yours all the way to Yuma, Lee," he said.

"I'll keep the door between us locked at all times," said Lee drily. "You've got a dirty mind, Jack."

Jack grinned. "Just interested in the interplay between a predatory female and a real stud like yourself, Lee."

"You honor me," murmured Lee.

"I go now," said Queho.

Lee nodded.

"Where I sleep, Kershaw?"

Lee jerked a thumb back toward the cabin. "In there."

Queho looked at Mellen.

Mellen shook his head. "No, Kershaw," he said firmly.

Lee flicked the ashes from the end of his cigar. His gray eyes took on the blue ones of Jack Mellen. "I paid first-class passage for two," he reminded the skipper.

"No, Kershaw," repeated Mellen. "Personally, I don't give a goddamn if you want the breed in there with you, but the company won't allow it, and you know that as well as I do."

"He'll freeze his ass off on the freight deck, Jack!"

"I'll refund your money," said Jack.

Lee turned to speak to the breed, but Queho was gone. He looked down to the wharf and saw the breed walking silently toward the shore. "Can you imagine how he must feel?" asked Lee.

"Dammit, Kershaw! I don't make the rules! Why must you flaunt your damned tolerance in everyone's faces?"

Lee shrugged. "*¿Quien sabe?* He works well with me. He saved my life. I can depend on him, which is perhaps the most important of all. I suppose he's the next thing to a true friend."

"What is he anyway? Half Paiute?"

Kershaw relighted his cigar. "They say his mother was the product of a drunken Mexican teamster and a half-witted Mohave Apache squaw, and some say she was half

21

Chemehuevis, which is about the next thing to a Southern Paiute, but don't ever say that to *him*. He's proud of the Mohave Apache blood."

"And his father?"

"His father was a trooper when Negro cavalry were stationed here for a short time. He was a mulatto, or a quadroon, or an octaroon, but to the Army he was a nigger, and so was enlisted into a black unit. How the hell they classify such mixed white and black blood is beyond me."

"So, in a sense, he's not really a *half*-breed then?"

Lee smiled faintly. "Classifying, eh, Jack?"

Milly Felding appeared at the top of the ladder, followed by her puffing husband and the gaggle of luggage-carrying troopers.

"They say he deliberately missed that shot at Ahvote," suggested Mellen.

Lee shook his head. "No one can ever know that. He had no love for Ahvote. Besides, it was almost an impossible shot. You could have seen that had you been there, Jack."

"But *you* hit Ahvote! The story of that shot has traveled all over the Territory. You're a legend in your own time, Kershaw!"

Lee waved a casual hand. "Dumb luck," he said quietly.

"Well, Kershaw!" cried Will Felding jovially. "We're to be neighbors, I see!"

"All the way to Yuma," said Lee drily. He tipped his hat to Milly Felding and her great blue eyes widened as she smiled. She was an artist with those guileless-looking eyes. "Mister Kershaw can entertain us with his tales of manhunting, I'm sure," she said.

"He never talks about them, ma'am," put in Mellen.

"But he must! He's famous now, Captain Mellen."

Lee almost gagged. He turned away and looked toward the shore. The sun was gone now. The lights of the post winked on through the gathering darkness, and the lights of the steamer twinkled on the wind-driven waves like watered silk ribbon. There would be no more passengers.

Will Felding closed the door behind himself and his wife. The troopers walked toward the ladder. "You see that ass of hers, Charley?" one of the troopers asked another one. "Who could miss it?" retorted Charley. The troopers were still laughing when they reached the freight deck.

"Have to check the repair work," said Jack. "We leave at first light of dawn." His feet thudded on the ladder.

Lee Kershaw stood alone on the windswept deck with the tip of his cigar alternately lighting his face as he drew in on the weed or plunging it again into shadow as the tip dimmed away. Queho was taking a hell of a long time to get the rest of the gear.

Lee went into his cabin. He could hear the voices of Will and Milly Felding from the next cabin through the thin connecting door. Milly's rather shrill, petulant voice was overriding the deeper tones of her husband. It seemed she wasn't too happy with the accommodations.

Lee lighted the gimbaled lamp and felt about in one of his bags for a brandy bottle. He drank deeply and then again to take his mind off his aching shoulder. There was a good army surgeon down at Fort Yuma; an expert on knife and gunshot wounds. He was the real reason Lee was going downriver.

He stripped to the waist and eyed in the mirror his lean upper body with the faint whitish lines of knife scars and a few puckered bullet holes. None of them had taken so long to heal as the one that bothered him now. He heard the faint ringing of the dinner gong as he changed undershirt and shirt. He shrugged a little painfully into his coat and selected a few long nines, which he placed in his coat pocket. He eyed himself in the mirror. A lean and saturnine-looking face stared back at him with hard gray eyes, a startling contrast to the brown mahogany of his face and the reddish brown beard and mustache. "*Bien parecido*," said Kershaw to himself. He grinned as he blew out the lamp and left the cabin.

Queho stood at the after end of the hurricane deck and watched Lee enter the little dining salon behind the pilothouse. He hurriedly brought the saddles to the cabin and dumped them on the floor. He lighted a match and found a brandy bottle. He drank again and again, his throat working convulsively. He wiped his thick lips, grinned, and drank again and again.

FIVE

"*YOU CAME WEST* with the Army I believe, Kershaw?" asked Will Felding as he mounded the mashed potatoes on his plate and scooped out a hollow on the top. He reached for the gravy boat and neatly topped the hollow with the thick, brown fluid.

"No," replied Lee. "Born and bred in New Mexico Territory."

"But you did serve, eh?"

Lee nodded. "One hitch was enough, Colonel."

"They say you scouted for a time?"

"For a time," agreed Lee. He kept looking at Felding to avoid the rather intent stare in Mildred Felding's too large baby-blue eyes. "I didn't like hunting and killing Indians."

"I could have sworn you served longer than one hitch," continued Felding.

Jack Mellen shoved back his plate. "He did," he said drily. "But not in the United States Army."

Felding looked up quickly. "Eh? What does that mean?"

Lee smiled. "In Mexico," he said. "Sonora, Chihuahua, Coahuila, and a few other places."

"You mean—in the *Mexican* Army?" asked Mildred.

"Not exactly," replied Lee. "If you mean the *Federales*."

Jack grinned widely. "He means—*against* the Mexican Army."

Felding's jaw dropped. "A revolutionary?" he asked.

"A hired gun," replied Lee. "A gringo mercenary, if you will."

25

"Well, I'll be damned!" cried Felding. "You hear that, Milly?"

"Oh, Mister Kershaw has done *so* many romantic things!" she cooed.

"Not exactly," corrected Lee. "The pay was good, and in gold, when I got it. Seems like I never quite picked the right revolution."

Felding emptied his plate and refilled it. "But it's the man hunting in which you've made a name for yourself, eh, Kershaw?"

Lee nodded. He took out a long nine and looked at Milly. She nodded. "I love the smell of a good cigar," she said. Felding looked quickly at her, his filled fork halfway to his mouth. "You've never said that to me, Mildred," he accused.

Lee lighted the cigar over the top of the lamp. He was almost tempted to get off the steamer right then and there and wait for the next one, and if his shoulder hadn't been bothering him too much he would have done it.

"You're known from one end of the Southwest to the other as the best manhunter in the business, Kershaw," rumbled Felding.

Lee casually waved his cigar.

"He knows it too," said Jack drily.

Lee grinned. "Professional pride," he countered.

"How romantic!" cried Milly. "Man hunting man!"

"The most dangerous game in the world," said Lee quietly.

Felding waved a sceptre composed of his fork stabbed through a dripping piece of beef. "But you've never failed to bring in your man, eh, Kershaw?"

"Oh, Will," put in Milly. "It's sometimes dead or alive, isn't it, Mister Kershaw? I mean—you *don't* have to bring them in alive, do you?"

"I try," replied Lee. "I do not take on assignments where it is stated they want them dead or alive."

Felding shook his head. "It seems to me that it would be

much less expensive, plus the bother of bringing a man to trial after months of feeding him and quartering him, then the wages of the manhunter, the guards, the other personnel involved, sir! How much easier to put a bullet into your quarry and report that he resisted arrest, eh, Kershaw?"

It was very quiet in the little salon, except for the dry scrabbling of the night wind about the superstructure of the steamer and the steady, powerful masticating of Felding's teeth.

"Eh, Kershaw?" asked Felding at last as he swallowed his food.

"That would make me judge, jury, and executioner, sir," quietly replied Lee. "I *hunt* men. I do not judge them, *or* execute them."

Felding narrowed his eyes. "You're cheese-paring now, Kershaw."

"Do you still have my husband's rifle, Mister Kershaw?" asked Milly, to change the dangerous subject.

"It is *my* rifle, ma'am," replied Lee.

"I still want it as a trophy, sir," put in Felding. "I should never have put it up as a bet on that poker game."

No, you sonofabitch, thought Lee, because you never thought you'd lose it.

"I can offer you a good price," said Felding.

Lee shook his head. "By the way," he asked, "did you ever get your tobacco jar?"

Felding bobbed his head up and down as he cut into his meat. "Neatly cleaned by the post surgeon. The blacksmith cut off the top and hinged it. Mildred lined it with wine-treated deerskin." He smiled proudly at his young wife. "I have it in my cabin," he added. "Would you like to see it?"

"Not particularly," Lee said quietly.

Mildred Felding focused her great blue eyes on the enigmatic face of the man named Kershaw. Will was too slowwitted to understand Lee's reply, but *she* wasn't.

"A fine rifle that," said Felding. "By God! I've fired a few matches with it and never lost a one, but I've never seen a shot like that one you made that day, Kershaw."

27

"Keep it up, sweetheart," urged Mildred, "and he'll never part with that rifle you want so much."

Felding mopped up his plate with a piece of bread. "Perhaps it is only sentimentality, Kershaw, but because that rifle, and yourself of course, saved my sweet Milly's life that day, I'd like to have it."

"In that case," said Lee drily, "you'd have to have me along with it."

Felding quickly raised his head to stare at Lee, then caught the joke. He guffawed, and a big piece of gravy bread caught in his throat. He bent forward, choking and gasping, his fat face turning a purplish red. Lee was out of his chair like a cat. A powerful hand hit Felding in the middle of his fat back, and he spat out the bread onto his plate. He raised a tear-streaming face. "Thanks, Kershaw!" he gasped.

"Por nada," replied Lee as he sat down. He saw the look of disgust on Mildred's face as she looked at her husband.

"The rifle," reminded Felding. "I'll double my offer."

"The money would mean nothing to me," said Lee.

"Every man has his price," reminded Mildred.

"No," corrected Lee. "There are still some men left who have no price."

"Like you?" she asked.

He stood up. "I didn't say so."

"Poker tonight?" asked Jack Mellen to change the subject.

"You're on," put in Felding.

"Lee?" asked Mellen.

"I have some reading to do," said Lee. "Good night." He turned and left the salon.

"That goddamned snob!" snapped Mildred in fury.

"Who? Kershaw?" asked Mellen in surprise.

"I wasn't talking to you," she said.

"Sorry," said Mellen. He stood up. "My chief engineer will join us for a game, Colonel." He left the salon cabin.

"That goddamned snob!" repeated Mildred.

"Who? Mellen?" asked Felding in surprise.

"No! That Kershaw! Him and his airs! Who the hell does he think he is?"

"I never thought of him like that," mused Felding as he reached for his dessert.

"You never think about him in any way! The man is two-faced!"

Felding looked at her. "How so?" he asked.

"Haven't you noticed how he looks at me?"

Felding slowly placed his fork on his plate. "What do you mean?" he slowly asked.

"Those that have eyes can see," she said archly.

"Mildred, if you have such accusations you had better be sure of them," he admonished her.

"Forget it!" she said. She stood up. "Are you going to sit there all night?"

"Poker," he reminded her.

"And you'll sit up all night drinking, leaving me alone in that damned tiny cabin?"

He stood up. "Why no! Not if you wish me to come with you."

She shook her head. "Enjoy yourself," she said. "You'd be no good to me or any other woman with all that whiskey you plan to drink."

"I only thought that we'd be awakened early by the sounds of the steamer leaving and that you might want your beauty sleep."

She leaned over and patted his fat face. "Of course, Will! Stupid of me not to think of that. You're a good man, Will, and a fine husband." She pecked a kiss at his fat face and left the cabin.

Will Felding sat down heavily and looked curiously at the door. He shook his head and attacked his dessert.

SIX

QUEHO SQUATTED WITH his back against the bulkhead, eating lower-deck fare from a tin plate resting on his muscular thighs. "Everything here, Kershaw," he said. He picked up his food with his hands and gnawed at it, but his curious eyes were on Lee.

Lee nodded. He sat down on his bunk and reached into his bag for a brandy bottle. The level was far lower than it had been when he had last drunk from it. "Where will you sleep?" he asked.

Queho shrugged. "*¿Quien sabe?*"

"Come up here in a couple of hours after everyone else is asleep. No one will know. The skipper and the colonel are in for an all-night poker session. They'll only leave the table long enough to piss over the railing."

"You sell rifle to fat man?"

Lee took a drink and shook his head. He was getting tired of talking about that damned rifle. It really didn't mean that much to him. He was basically a Winchester man.

"He still want rifle, eh?"

"I said I would not sell it."

Queho stood up and placed his plate on the table. He wiped his greasy hands on his thighs. "You pay me salary in cash, you say. How much, Kershaw?"

Lee shrugged. "Hundred dollars a month and food."

"*Enju!* How much you want for rifle?"

Lee studied the dark, scarred face of the breed. "Not you too?"

Queho nodded. "Look, Kershaw, you keep rifle for yourself and not pay me until rifle paid for, then you give to me."

"It would take months."

"No matter."

The face of the breed was broad, with the characteristic high cheekbones of his Indian blood, while his acquiline nose flared out curiously at the base into the flared nostrils of the Negro. The lips were negroid and his beard, a poor imitation of Lee's, was scraggly like an Indian's and kinky like a Negro's. It was the eyes that gave the man his curious look—the light eyes of the Caucasian.

"Well?" asked Queho.

"You know this type of rifle is not for you, Queho," said Lee quietly.

"Why not!"

"It's not practical."

"I can shoot it good as you. Maybe better, goddamnit!"

Lee nodded. "That is possible," he agreed. "But you could have hit Ahvote with it that day, and yet you did not. You could have made a damned hero out of yourself that day, Queho. Why didn't you?"

"Because no one would make a hero out of a dirty breed, Kershaw. You know that."

Lee nodded. "Which brings us back to the rifle, Queho. How long do you think some white men would let you keep such a rifle? You ask for the truth. That's the truth! The rifle is not for you. Don't try to compete with white men in this country, Queho. Granted, you're as good a man as any of them, and maybe better than most, but you are not *white!*"

"I no anything! I no white! I no red! I no black! What the hell am I, Kershaw? You wise. Maybe *you* tell me?"

Lee drank a little. "You know I can't do that," he replied.

After a little while, the breed left the cabin and closed the door behind himself.

Lee shrugged. He stripped to his long-johns and raised the lampwick a little. He selected a thin, leather-clad book from his little library, placed the brandy bottle near at hand, lighted a fresh cigar, and settled himself in his bunk for some serious reading.

The cabin was pitch dark when Lee awoke to the sound of the inter-cabin doorhandle being gently tried. He raised his head. It swam a little from the brandy fumes. He could hear Queho breathing softly in the upper bunk. The doorhandle was turned again. Something clicked sharply in the lock. The door creaked gently as it opened. The full figure of Mildred Felding was silhouetted through the diaphanous negligee she wore by the soft lamplight behind her. The scent of her perfume came to Lee. She came softly toward him, holding out a hand. "Oh, Lee," she said tenderly. The mattress creaked in the upper bunk, and Queho turned to look over the side of the bunk full into the startled woman's face. She saw the dark, sweat-streaked skin, glistening in the lamplight, and the strange, light-colored eyes staring, as though a demon were peering at her with evil intentions through a smoky window of hell itself. "Oh, my God!" she screamed. Queho cursed. He had been as startled as she had been. He reached down and clamped a hand over her gaping mouth as she drew in full lungpower to scream again. She sank her sharp teeth into his hand and jerked her head backward. In an effort to free his hand he rolled over the side of the bunk and his free hand caught at the front of her negligee to save his falling. The thin, sweat-damp material ripped freely from shoulder to belly. Her great breasts, dewed with sweat, swung freely as she turned to flee.

Lee cursed softly as he thrust out his head from beneath the upper bunk. Queho was down on his knees, right in Lee's way. Lee shoved at him. Queho clawed out at the woman; his hands caught at the ruin of her negligee where it hung over her broad hips. Queho tore the material down about her plump legs and saw her wide, glistening white rump. "Jesus God!" he yelled in drunken fervor.

Milly ran toward her cabin, missed the door, hit the bulkhead, and seemed to rebound back into the room, striking her heavy rump against Queho's down-bent head as he tried to get up, driving him back against Lee. Lee pushed past the breed and stood up. Queho wrapped an arm about the woman's waist. Lee tore it loose, and Queho drove upward from the deck. His head caught Lee hard under the chin, and smashed him backward against the cabin door, which flew open. Lee landed flat on his back on the outer deck. The woman was screaming like one of the Furies, never seeming to run out of breath.

Feet thudded on the deck. Will Felding led the charge from the dining salon, followed by Jack Mellen and Jim Anderson, the big chief engineer. A heel caught Lee alongside the jaw as he tried to rise. He gripped the leg and upended Will Felding on the deck in front of Mellen and Anderson, and both men sprawled over the falling agent.

Lee jumped into the cabin and tried to separate Queho and the shrieking woman. Queho hit Lee, driving him back against Will Felding, who was just coming in through the doorway. Felding shoved Lee aside and snatched at Lee's loaded Colt lying on the table. He cocked it and whirled to fire into Queho's face. Lee knocked the Colt to one side and the six-gun exploded alongside his head, half deafening him and temporarily blinding him. A man coughed hard behind Lee. He whirled to see the engineer staggering backward from the short-range impact of the soft-lead, 200-grain bullet. He hit the rail and went over backward, to crash down into the shallow water between the side of the *Mohave* and the shore.

Will Felding smashed the smoking Colt across Lee's face and drove him back against the wall. The Colt exploded again, and the slug creased the side of Queho's head, driving him unconscious to the deck. Lee went down on his knees, covering his blood-streaming face with his hands. The Colt came down atop his head and drove him flat on his face on the deck. The last two things he remembered were someone shoving the Colt into his right hand and the incessant banshee-shrieking of the woman.

SEVEN

THE DISTANT MOUNTAINS seemed to smoke in the infernal temperature. They appeared to move slowly and sinuously in the shifting, wavering veils of heated air, as though they had a primitive life-form of their own. They were leaden-hued and wrinkled, like the thick hides of huge prehistoric beasts half-buried in the harsh soil of the dessert that lapped at their bases and flanks. The desert itself was almost pool-table flat and almost naked of growth, except for a few metallic-looking plants that had somehow learned to survive in that land of hellfire. Shallow washes wove themselves in braided fashion across the heat-shimmering expanse of the desert.

In direct contrast to the erratic courses of the washes was the road at right angles to them. It was as straight as a bowstring and seemed to come from nowhere through the distant haze to vanish into nothing but more heat haze. The road itself was the only sign of man in that sun-cursed and empty land. There seemed to be no life on the desert or the mountains. It was the very core of the summer heat in the hottest summer known to the memory of the few men who had ever lived there. At that time of the year, the only movements usually seen were the shifting, writhing veils of disturbed air. There was, that one burning summer day, however, two other movements rare indeed in that land where heat and lack of water killed men. One of the movements was that of a thin wraith of saffron-hued dust rising from the road and moving so slowly it seemed hardly to move at all. The other movement was the slow rise and fall of the deep chest of the man who squatted in the very center of a wide wash that crossed the road. There was no shelter there from the full-burning stroke of the killer sun. A limp cigarette dangled from the man's thick lips. His curiously light-colored eyes were slitted against the reflected glare of the sun from the whitish caliche that paved the wash, and his sweat-greased hat was pulled low over his eyebrows. His elbows rested on his lean but powerful thighs, and his strong hands, dirty-nailed and corded, hung loosely between his bent knees. In the scant shade of his body there lay a well-worn Winchester '73 rifle polished with deer fat, and an almost empty bottle of rotgut whiskey. The temperature was hovering at 110 degrees in the shade.

Time seemed to stand still. The dust rose higher in the windless air, until at last the vehicle could be seen under it—an Abbott-Downing stagecoach drawn by four dusty, red-mouthed mules. The Concord coach swayed on its great leather thoroughbraces as the road dipped and sagged into the many dry washes, sometimes disappearing from sight, like a small vessel sinking into a deep wavetrough, only to emerge slowly into view again on the next rise before once again plunging down out of sight.

Soon the intermingled sounds of the approaching coach came to the waiting man in the wash, and his incredibly acute hearing picked out each individual sound, as a music-lover concentrates on picking out the part of each orchestral instrument in a complicated symphony. There was the steady thudding of sixteen hoofs; the slapping of the sweat-lathered harness; the strident jingling of the tracechains; the dull clucking of the sandboxes; the soft, greasy chuckling of the hubs; the hissing of the slim wheels on the hard sand of the road, and the occasional pistol-cracking report of the jehu's whip.

Slowly, the waiting man raised his faded bandanna to mask his dark, scarred face, leaving only a narrow slit for his curious-looking eyes.

The coach was close now. It dipped out of sight just beyond the wash. The man stood up with his Winchester hanging loosely in his hands athwart the upper part of his thighs. The lead mules showed up and plunged down into the wash, followed by the wheel mules and the swaying, lurching coach. The driver touched the brake to slow the descent of the vehicle. One of the lead mules caught the spoor of the masked man and snorted in warning, but too late.

The Winchester cracked flatly and the shot echo rolled evenly across the desert. Gunsmoke wreathed about the masked man, as the driver braked hard and drew in on the ribbons to halt the excited team. The brakes shrieked hoarsely and puffed out stinking friction smoke as the coach lurched to a crazy halt in the middle of the wash. The bitter yellow dust swirled on past the coach and mingled with the white gunsmoke drifing about the silent, masked man standing in front of the lead mules.

A woman screamed from within the coach. It was a familiar scream to the masked man. He had an excellent memory.

The driver quickly wrapped the ribbons about the brakehandle and raised his hands. He uneasily eyed the eerie-looking figure of the masked man, half-seen through the dust and gunsmoke as though he were a phantom figure not of this earth. There was a double-barreled, sawed-off ten-gauge shotgun lying at the driver's feet and a holstered six-gun at his side, but he was not stupid enough to make a move for either one of them.

It was very quiet except for the harsh breathing of the mules.

"There ain't no registered mail or bullion on this rig," volunteered the driver.

The curious looking light-colored eyes seemed to slide sideways to look at the coach.

"They's only three passengers—all wimmen; all for Prescott."

The masked man nodded. "I know," he said.

The driver was puzzled. He looked beyond the masked man. There was no sign of a horse. There was not even the faint comfort of a trail across the empty desert land.

"Tell them to get out," ordered the bandit.

The driver clambered down. As his feet struck the ground, he felt his six-gun being plucked from his holster, although he had not heard the sound of feet on the hard ground. He glanced down between his legs to see the toetips of dusty moccasins, and an uneasy feeling crawled up his sweating back. The driver opened the coach door. "Sorry, ladies," he said. "You'll have to get out."

Amy, an auburn-haired prostitute, was the first to get out of the coach. "Must be hot behind that mask, mister," she cracked. Her little joke fell flatly in the quietness. Mildred Felding clambered out next. She had put on some weight while summering in San Francisco. "You won't get away with this, mister," she said, as she tried to stare down the masked man.

"Seems like I am," the masked man said laconically.

"You know who I am?" she demanded.

He nodded. "Mrs. Felding," he replied. "Wife of *Colonel* Will Felding, special agent for Indian Bureau. You been in Frisco since about May, getting better from attack on *Mohave*." His voice was strangely muffled and distorted behind the damp bandanna that masked his face.

Mildred Felding narrowed her eyes. "You'll find yourself in deep trouble for this, mister!" she snapped.

"I'm *in* deep trouble," he countered.

Lucille, the slim, flat-chested, dark-haired favorite niece of the Governor of Arizona Territory, was the last one out of the coach. She had been called from her schooling in San Francisco to take over the Prescott household of her recently widowed uncle. Luckily, Mildred Felding had agreed to leave early for Prescott to chaperone Lucille during the long trip by sea, river, and coach to the Territorial capital. Maybe it hadn't been so lucky after all, thought the girl, and she hadn't learned to like Mrs. Felding one little bit during the long trip.

"Maybe all he wants are our purses, honey," soothed Amy.

"The Three Fates," drily commented the masked man.

"You've been reading books," accused Amy.

He shook his head. "Smart cellmate tell me about such things."

"The sun is hell on these ladies," reminded the driver.

"Sun is hell on whole goddamned country," corrected the bandit.

"Don't I know you?" asked Mildred.

"Dump luggage in road," ordered the bandit.

The three women stood together in the hot shade of the coach as the driver emptied out the boot.

"I *said* we should have had an escort, driver!" barked Mildred.

"Weren't none," said the driver. "Most of 'em was out chasin' someone." He slanted his eyes toward the masked man. "Seems like they were chasin' in the wrong direction."

"Well, where was our guard?"

The driver shrugged. "Got drunk last night. Got a knife between his shoulder blades. No one knows who done it. Couldn't find anyone else willin' to come along." He slid his eyes sideways again toward the bandit.

The masked man touched a small suitcase with a moccasined toe. "Each woman take one this size. Take only what you need. Long way to go."

They stood there looking uncomprehendingly at him. The prostitute looked out across the desert toward the distant mountains, which appeared to smoke in the intense heat. "Where?" she asked uneasily.

"*Now!*" ordered the masked man.

They obediently opened their luggage and threw out the unnecessary items. Mildred opened a light traveling trunk.

39

"These gowns came all the way from Paris," she said petulantly.

"Won't wear well in mountains," said the bandit. He reached inside the boot and brought out a long, polished wooden case made of the finest Philippine mahogany and fitted with German-silver hardware.

Mildred watched him out of the corners of her eyes as she began to pack a small suitcase. She was almost sure now who he was. Trouble was, she didn't *want* to be sure.

Lucille sobbed. She inelegantly wiped her nose with the back of a hand.

"Take it easy, kid," soothed Amy. "He's only a man."

"Fine advice," sneered Mildred, "but then, you've had a great deal of experience with such men, haven't you, *honey?*"

"And I got paid for it," drily admitted Amy. "What did *you* get out of it, *honey?*"

"Unhitch mules and hold them," ordered the bandit. "When you last water them? How much water left?"

The driver wiped the sweat from his face with a forearm. "They was a fresh team twenty miles back. They're about due for water now. I've got two big mule-canteens for them and two smaller ones inside for the ladies. That's it, mister."

The masked man swung up to the driver's seat. He reached under the seat and held up a small canteen filled with water. "Maybe you forgot this, eh?" he asked.

The driver shrugged. He was midway on his long and lonely desert run. It was twenty miles back to the swing station, but he had used about the last of the water there. The water wagon wasn't due in there until the next day. It was another fifteen miles to the end of the stage, and water. The next water south of the road was forty miles away. To the north of the road were the mountains, and if there was any water in there in the summertime only the Paiutes and the Hualapais knew where it was, and they never went in there during the summer. It was an evil place.

The three women finished packing and stood close together in the hot shade of the coach. "Each of you get up on a mule," ordered the masked man. They each clambered awkwardly up onto a mule, aided by the driver. Mildred's modish traveling skirt hiked way up, to reveal a plump calf encased in smooth silk. "It's been a long time since I've ridden like this," observed Amy. No one paid any attention to her.

The masked man stood looking down at the polished gun-case at his feet. "Get shotgun," he ordered the driver over his shoulder.

The driver climbed up to the seat and placed his sweating, trembling hands on the Greener. It was loaded with Blue Whistlers holding 00 shot, and the wads had been split—enough power to take off the bandit's head at fifteen feet.

"Don't try it," warned the masked man without turning.

The Greener hit the ground. The bandit turned and bent to pick it up, and as he did so his dirty, sweat-slick bandanna slipped from his dark, scarred face.

"Jesus God," breathed the driver, and he was immediately sorry he had done so.

"Get down," ordered the bandit as he pulled up his mask. "You know me, eh?"

The driver shook his head. He had been afraid many times before in his life but with nothing like the fear that chilled him now.

The bandit cut lengths of the coach reins to fashion lead-ropes for the mules ridden by the women. He made a sling for the shotgun and hung it on the last mule. "Get the mules' canteens. Water the mules," he ordered the driver.

The driver hung the nose-buckets on the mules and filled the buckets from the big canteens, never taking his eyes from the bandit.

The bandit squatted in front of the polished wooden case and unsnapped the German-silver catches. He raised the lid to look down into the fitted interior. A heavy single-shot

Sharps M1874 rested in its velvet-covered receptacle. The sun seemed to make little trickles of bluish-tinted fire as it reflected from the new gold-and-silver-filled engraving about the breech of the fine rifle. It bounced bright rays from the polished silver plate fastened in the center of the inside of the lid. *"Enju,"* said the masked man.

"What does that mean?" asked Amy, low-voiced, of the driver.

The driver looked nervously up at her. "It means 'good'," he hoarsely replied.

"In what language?"

The driver looked at the bandit, whose full interest focused on the rifle and the fittings inside the wooden case.

"Well?" demanded Mildred impatiently.

"Apache," said the driver at last.

Mildred was not daunted. "That is my property, *you,"* she informed the bandit. "I had it specially engraved, and that case made for it in San Francisco. It is for my husband . . ." Her voice died away as the curious, light eyes of the bandit fixed themselves on her.

"Keep your mouth shut," hissed Amy out of the side of her mouth.

"I know him," informed the bandit. "I know how you got rifle. I know who it really belongs to. *You* know, woman?"

"Well, it was originally my husband's, and he lost it at poker to a man named Kershaw. Personally, I think Kershaw cheated at cards. I got it back for my husband."

"Kershaw?" asked Amy. "Lee Kershaw? I know him!"

"That doesn't surprise me," sneered Mildred, "knowing the both of you for what you are."

"How Kershaw lose this gun, woman?" demanded the masked man.

Mildred opened, then closed her usually ready mouth. "You tell me, eh?"

"Well, it was confiscated from his belongings when he

was sentenced to Yuma Pen. I managed to get it. *Repossess* it, I should say."

The man tapped the engraved breech of the rifle. "What it say here?"

"Ahvote. April, 1881," replied the woman.

"And here?" He tapped the plate inside the lid.

"Colonel Will Felding from his beloved wife Mildred, August, 1881."

"But it should say Lee Kershaw, eh, woman?"

There was no reply.

The masked man passed a dirty hand over the fittings in the case, the long Vollmer telescope, the vernier-tang sight, the globe-front sight, the brass-tipped wooden wiping rod, the capper, the bullet-starter, and the other accouterments and polished tools. He picked up and shook the brass powder-can. It was full. He opened the primer box to find it full. He opened the bullet-box to count at least fifty grooved and greased 370-grain paper-patched bullets. There was a roll of bank-note paper for further patching. He opened the long box of cartridge cases and stared down at the three two- and one-quarter-inch long brass cases. He looked up slowly at the woman. "Where are the other cartridge cases?" he demanded.

She was startled. "Well, they must all be there!"

"Only *three?*"

"I don't know about those things!" she cried.

He stood up, and his strong black-nailed hands opened and closed spasmodically. "Only three?" he yelled insanely. For a moment they all thought he was going to attack the woman; then he suddenly, almost too suddenly, calmed down. "All right," he said. "Maybe get more. Maybe three enough." He closed the lid of the box and snapped it shut. He fashioned a leather sling for the case and hung it on the mule opposite the shotgun.

The driver finished watering the mules. He took off the nose-buckets and walked to the coach with them and the two big canteens.

The masked man walked to the coach and opened a door. He reached inside and ripped up the worn upholstery with his powerful talon-like hands tipped by dirty, ragged fingernails. He thumb-snapped a match into flame and dropped it into one of the holes in the seat. A wisp of smoke quickly arose. In a little while, the fire was crackling merrily away as it ate swiftly into the horsehair stuffing and the worn leather. The smoke drifted from the windows and rose string-straight into the quiet air.

"That smoke can be seen for miles," warned Amy. "You'll give yourself away."

He looked at her. "Who's to see it?" he asked.

He had her there.

"Any water left in canteens?" asked the bandit.

The driver shook his head.

"Hang the other canteens on my mule."

"You sure no water in mule canteens?" asked the masked man again.

The driver turned from the mule and nodded.

"Enju! Start walking, mister."

The driver held out his hands, palms upward. "Where?" he asked piteously.

The masked man mounted his mule and sat it, looking down at the driver. "Take your choice," he carelessly replied. He looked toward the distant, heat-hazed mountains.

"I'll never make it to water! Takes three gallons a day for a man to walk in this damned heat! At least give me one canteen, mister!"

"Shit!" said the masked man. He led the three mules slowly up the wash.

"No living man can make it to water from here without a canteen!" yelled the driver.

"I can," said the bandit over his shoulder.

The driver stood amidst the gathering smoke. "I know who you are!" he yelled foolishly.

The Winchester '73 cracked four times, almost as fast as

the action could be described. The mule canteens jumped sideways and clattered to the ground, each of them neatly holed twice through by .44/40 slugs. The water ran from them into the thirsty ground before the driver could reach them to stop the flow. "God damn you to hell!" the driver shouted hoarsely.

There was no reply from the masked man.

In a little while, only a thread of saffron-hued dust moved across the heat-shimmering desert between the road and the infernal mountains.

EIGHT

AMY'S MULE STUMBLED and went down with the sound of a dry stick being snapped. Amy threw a long and shapely leg over the back of the mule and stepped clear of him as he went down. The mule struggled to get up, but his left frong leg was cleanly broken. Amy took her suitcase and sat down on it.

The masked man walked easily back to the downed mule. He gripped the halter and suddenly twisted the mule's head up and to one side. The razor edge of his knife sliced cleanly through the throat muscles, and he stepped quickly backward to avoid the sudden gushing of the dark blood. The women watched him in horrified fascination as he squatted beside the still quivering hulk of the mule and hacked out a square of the dusty hide. Darkness grew in the heat-soaked canyon as he worked. The only sounds were the blowing of the tired mules and the ripping of the knife through hide and flesh. Dripping chunks of the bloody meat were placed on the square of hide.

"Why?" asked Amy at last.

He looked sideways at her. "Good mule meat sweeter than pork," he replied.

"To a gut-eating Apache or a breed," sneered Mildred.

He looked at her over the upper edge of the bandanna. "You be eating some of this before too long and be damned thankful for it," he said.

"God forbid!" she cried.

"We'll see," he promised.

46

"Don't I know you?" she asked suspiciously.

"You should," he said over his shoulder.

"Some saloon or whorehouse?" sweetly asked Amy.

The masked man shrugged.

Mildred took her courage in hand. She snatched at the bandanna and it fell free from the man's face. He did not turn. "I think I know you," she said quietly. He turned and looked up at her. *"Queho!"* she screamed.

"That, was a mistake," warned Amy. "The driver knew who he was. You saw what happened to him."

"The breed from Prescott and Fort Mohave," said Mildred.

Queho wiped the greasy sweat from his dark face. "What breed, woman?" he demanded. "Half-breed? Quarter-breed? Maybe *all*-breed, eh, woman?"

It was almost as though the woman was talking to herself as she mechanically replied: "Part Mohave Apache, part half-breed Mexican, and part white man."

He stood up and wiped his strong, bloody hands on the greasy thighs of his filthy trousers. "Maybe you forgot *nigger* too, eh, woman?"

"That too," she agreed.

He grinned, but there was no true mirth on his strange face. "So, what you call me now, eh, woman?"

"But you were sent to Yuma Pen with Kershaw for twenty years!"

He grinned. "Only few months. I no like it there. So I left."

"No man has ever escaped from Yuma Pen and lived to talk about it," said Amy wisely.

He wrapped the hide about the meat and fastened it with a long strip of the hide. "I did," he said matter of factly. "Get on mules," he ordered.

"There are only three left," said Amy.

He looked at Mildred. "You walk, woman."

"I won't be able to keep up!" she cried.

They all mounted except Mildred. "Follow the canyon

for three more miles," said Queho. "We'll stop for the night there." He kicked his mule in the ribs and led the other two mules up the dark canyon. Lucille's mule was badly lamed.

"I won't be able to keep up!" foolishly repeated Mildred.

"What about water?" asked practical Amy. "The canteens are empty."

He looked back at her. "Do you think even *me*, Queho, could live in here without water, woman?"

She had no answer for that question.

Mildred Felding stood there in the heat-soaked darkness with the hot, stinging sweat running down her tired body. Then she started up the canyon with a great swaying of her too broad hips. The heel snapped off from her left shoe. She went down on her too plump knees and abraded them. She looked up the dark slot of the canyon. She could no longer see them. Her damp and stringy yellowish hair hung over her sweating face. She could hear her heart thudding violently against her ribs. She did not dare look back down the canyon. There was nothing back there but the unknown, but it was that which really frightened her.

NINE

THE FIRST ARIZONA posse sent out to check the nonarrival of the stagecoach found the driver lying face downward at the side of the road where the coarse sand was smooth. His sunburned hands were dug clawlike into the sand, as though he had intended dragging himself on his belly toward the water that was five miles away in the opposite direction. Traced in the sand just in front of his hands was a wavering scrawl of one word—*Queho*.

The deputy sheriff shaped a quirly and lighted it, cupping brown hands about the flame of the match to shield it from the dawn wind sweeping across the dry and empty land. "He got confused during the night, poor bastard," he said around the cigarette, "and was crawling back the way he came. Sam, you and Ellis load him on that spare horse and you take him back, Sam. Ellis, you and that Paiute come with me."

They rode north on the rutted road as the sun came up in a vast, silent explosion that changed the color-texture of the land from soft and mysterious gray tones into the bright, clashing colors that would show distinctly in the clear morning light until the day's heat changed them into vague, murderous tintings that seemed to harbor a hint of insanity.

"The next water is thirty miles ahead, Dan," warned Ellis.

"We've got water," said the deputy.

"It's more than twenty-five miles west to the river."

"We've got water," repeated Dan.

The stagecoach had burned down into a blackened heap of ashes and heat-warped metal. The deputy poked about in it with a boot-toe. He kicked out some of the blackened metal fittings. There were metal buttons, hinges, strap metal, curious-looking odds and ends, and some hooks and eyes. He picked up a thin lath of steel. "Corset stay," he said.

Ellis looked at the empty whiskey bottle in the wash. "He likely headed into the mountains, Dan."

Dan glanced at the two big blanket-covered canteens hanging from the saddles of the horses.

"If it really was Queho, we'll never catch him now, Dan."

Dan pointed at the faint mule tracks in the wash, then jerked a thumb toward them, looking at the Paiute tracker. The Paiute trotted up the wash. Dan followed, leading his horse and the tracker's.

"We just ain't got enough water to get to them mountains and back to water again!" yelled Ellis.

Dan turned. "There was three women in that coach," he said. He turned and followed the Paiute.

The Paiute stopped at the foot of the mountains under the full blaze of the noon sun. Beyond him was a great surface of smooth rock. The mule tracks had stopped where he stood.

"Go beyond the rocks," ordered Dan. "Cast about."

The Paiute did not move.

"*Vamonos!*" snapped Dan.

The Paiute did not "*vamonos.*"

"He's scared stiff," said Ellis.

"No water," croaked the Paiute.

"You lie!" accused Dan. "There must be water in there."

"It ain't the water. It's Queho," put in Ellis.

Dan slowly shaped a cigarette, keeping his eyes on the flat rock and the rising slopes of naked soil up above them, shimmering in the blaze of the sun. They had enough water in their canteens to reach the water in the mountains—if there *was* water in there. Only God, the Paiute, and Queho would know where that was, and none of the three of them were talking.

Dan lighted his cigarette and drew his Colt. He cocked it and pointed it at the head of the Paiute. *"Git!"* he ordered.

The Paiute did not *git*.

"He's more ascared of Queho then he is of you," said Ellis.

Slowly the Paiute stepped up on the rock.

The heavy rifle cracked flatly, distantly, and the big slug slapped into the head of Dan's horse with the sound of a stick being whipped into soft mud. The horse went down without making a sound.

High on the sun-cursed slopes, a wisp of smoke drifted off. Then the smoke was gone. The slopes seemed as barren as a lunar landscape.

Ellis raised his head a little from the ground. "It's Queho all right," he said, quite unnecessarily.

"How do you know?" Dan already knew the answer. Only two men he had ever known could shoot like that— Stalker and Queho.

"We'll have to go back now."

"We'll wait until dark."

"We'll be broiled to death by then."

Dan raised his head. The rifle promptly cracked. Gravel was flung stinging against the side of his face. He dropped his head. *"Jeeesus!* That was too damned close," he murmured.

"He could have hit you. He's warning us off."

"Christ, but I hate to give up!"

"What else can we do?"

"Go back, I guess. I'll take the Paiute's horse. The sonofabitch can walk."

The Paiute had already "walked."

TEN

"IT'S NO USE, Jim," argued Dan. "You won't get the Paiutes to go in there."

Sheriff Jim Hathaway had spread the map in the hot shade of a rock pinnacle. He looked at the emptiness of the map, marked by a few dotted, straggling lines that were supposed to be trails, and by a few (all too few) markings for waterholes neatly labeled, "Dry in summer. Water usually unfit to drink."

The second Arizona posse to start after Queho squatted in the shade of their horses, dragging on limp cigarettes, feeling the hot and itching sweat run down their bodies, and thinking always of cold beer. The Paiutes squatted sleepily in the full sunlight. Now and then one of them would raise his head a little to look at the hazy mountains. It was an evil place. The man the fool white men were hunting was not a man at all, but the fool white men would not admit that to themselves. The Paiutes knew.

Dan passed a hand across his burning eyes. "He's on the loose in an area of damned near five hundred square miles, south and east on the Arizona side and north and east of the Colorado on the Nevada side. The only water we can be sure of is in the river, twenty-five miles north, and twenty-five miles west."

"That ain't too bad," said Hathaway. "We can go north to the water and then follow the river where it curves to the south."

"We've got them damned mountains between us and the river either way we go. We don't know the passes, Jim."

"The Paiutes do."

"You'll never get them to show you."

"He has to leave a trail."

"He never leaves a trail."

"The mules and the three women will leave a trail. He can't avoid that, Dan."

"It's been a week since he held up the stagecoach."

"The women will have slowed him down."

"If they're still with him," said Dan.

Hathaway had no rebuttal for that one.

One of Paiutes pointed upward. A hawk had dived out of sight into a canyon.

"There's something dead up there," said the sheriff. He rolled up the map. "Damned useless thing this. My old blind granny could have made a better one using a pointed stick in the sand."

They sent the reluctant Paiutes on ahead by foot. They moved through the difficult terrain like wisps of wind driven smoke and just as noiselessly. They knew Queho had the hearing and sight of a wild animal.

They found the swollen mule carcass in a slot of a canyon. The stench of the escaping body-gases hung in the windless air like a noisome plague. Three of the legs stuck up stiffly from the obscenely bloated carcass, while the fourth leg was thrust out at an awkward angle. Something moved in a rotting hole gouged into a haunch. "Maggots," said Dan. "Now where the hell do *they* come from?"

The carcass moved as though in answer, easing out a fearsome puff of gas. The possemen moved quickly away.

"He's got meat for a week from that carcass," said Dan. "No wonder the breed sonofabitch can live in here."

"No water," said a Paiute, pointing up ahead.

"Queho went that way," said Dan. "He'd have to have water for himself, the women, and the mules." He unrolled the map and stabbed a blunt fingertip down on it. "There! Three miles ahead!"

"No water! Map no good!" insisted the Paiute.

"Kick their skinny asses up the canyon like a good boy, Danny," urged the sheriff.

The posse rode up the canyon with the dull sound of the hooves clashing metallically on the loose stones.

One of the Paiutes picked up the heel of a woman's shoe.

"Might be from a Paiute squaw's moccasin," joked one of the men.

"That ain't funny," rebuked the sheriff.

The map proved the Paiute wrong, at least about the water not being there. There *was* water there, about two feet of it, covered with a floating layer of green algae, which also coated the swollen hairy flanks of a dead mule lying centered in the rock pan. The men moved back from the stench.

Hathaway clipped and lighted a cigar. He looked at the two pack-burros, laden with oval-shaped water kegs. "We've still got enough water to reach the river," he said thoughtfully.

"Useless," argued Dan.

Hathaway thumb-snapped a lucifer to light his cigar. "We've got to go on, Dan" he said, between puffs on the cigar. "You saw that heel back there."

"They're raped and dead by now, Jim."

"You know who two of those women are?"

"Colonel Felding's spouse and the Governor's favorite niece."

Hathaway nodded. "Exactly."

"And a prostitute," added Dan as a second thought.

The rifle exploded on the heights. The men broke for cover. The rifle cracked again, sending its echo tumbling and bounding after the first echo. The lead burro stampeded up the canyon. The second burro lay dead on one crushed water-keg, while water from the other keg, now bullet-punctured, ran down his dusty hide to the ground. No one ventured out of cover to plug the hole.

Hathaway cautiously raised his head. The end of his cigar was a ragged ruin.

"You see now what I mean, Jim?" asked Dan.

Hathaway carefully pruned the end of his cigar with a pearl-handled penknife. "What the hell would he want three women for anyway?" he asked in general.

"A *mañada*," suggested Dan. "You know—brood mares, like a wild stud stallion keeps. Somewhere north of here, Queho likely is setting up his own little Eden—right in the center of a hell on earth."

Nothing moved on the heat-shimmering heights. The lead burro had vanished with the loaded water-kegs.

"You might be right, Danny," agreed Hathaway. "But just supposin' them three women won't play beddy-bye with him?"

Dan drew a finger across his brown throat.

Hathaway relighted his shortened cigar. "We'll never catch him this way," he said. "Besides, there's a Nevada posse working on the other side of the Colorado. Maybe they'll get him. We'll have to turn back now."

You ever see a Paiute grin? *They* did.

ELEVEN

THE NEVADA POSSE had worked upriver on the Nevada side until the narrow streak of shoreline had petered out. Beyond where they stood, with the water lapping at the sides of their boots, the river curved so that they could clearly see both sides of the gorge called "The Gut" by the rivermen. Here the river ran with a deceptive smoothness, deep and strong, with an undercurrent that could suck a man or horse down in a matter of seconds and hold them down, tumbling broken-boned along the rock-studded bottom, until the river let them up, perhaps five miles down the canyon, drowned and smashed to jelly, hardly recognizable as anything animal, vegetable, or mineral.

"You think he crossed the river, George?" a posseman asked of the deputy sheriff.

"*Here?* Hardly," replied George.

"Maybe he's still on the other side."

"No," said George. He raised his field glasses and focused them on a high point of the canyon wall on the Nevada side.

"How can you tell?"

George handed him the field glasses. "Take a look," he suggested. "That's him standing up there."

The four other possemen shrank back against the damp side of the gorge. George grinned. "Hell," he said, "if he had *wanted* to, he could have gotten all of us before we even saw where he was shooting from."

"He ain't got a rifle in his hands," said the man with the

glasses. "It's him all right. How the hell did he get across the river?"

"How the hell does he do anything, Les?" countered George.

"What about the women?" asked one of the possemen.

There was no answer. No one wanted to answer.

It was George who broke the silence. "If he left them on the Arizona side, it's Arizona's problem."

"I wasn't thinking about that," said the posseman who had asked the question.

"What do we do now, George?" asked Les.

George felt for the makings. "Go back," he replied. "We'll have to try and get at him from inland."

"So, maybe he'll cross the river again."

George shrugged as he shaped a cigarette. He handed the makings to Les. "Then he'll be Arizona's problem again."

"How does he live up there?" asked a posseman.

"Nothing lives up there except maybe lizards and hawks," said Les.

George lighted up. He looked over the flare of the match at the lone figure standing motionless on the heights watching them. "He does," he said quietly.

They turned the horses, with their hooves clashing on the pebbles and splashing in the water, in full view and good rifle range of the man on the heights.

Just before the canyon curved again, George looked back. The heights were empty. Shadows filled the gorge. The river roared sullenly. It was as though no one had ever lived there and never would.

TWELVE

"YOU COOK, WOMAN," said Queho to Mildred Felding.

She raised her head from where she lay on the cave floor, trembling with fatigue. She raised a dirty, broken-nailed hand and pushed back her stringy, dirty blond hair from her badly sunburned face. The wave had long gone from her hair, and her curling irons lay blackened in the ashes of the stagecoach more than thirty miles away, along with her heat-shattered bottles of pomade, cleansing lotions, perfumes and perfumed soaps, and her unguents and colognes.

"You hear?" demanded the breed.

"I'm not a damned squaw," she hotly protested.

A moccasined toe caught her just below the left ribs. She got up on her hands and knees. The flat of a moccasined sole caught her on the broad rump and drove her face downward on the floor of the cave. She covered her head with her arms as she was kicked unmercifully to her feet. She stumbled toward the fireplace at the side of the cave.

"I only tell you *once* when I want something," he said.

"Bastard," she said.

He nodded. "Bastard, yes, and *man* too!"

She was wise enough this time to keep her mouth shut.

Queho broke the shotgun he had taken from the stagecoach. He ejected the brass cartridges and ran a swab through the twin barrels. He snapped shut the breech and placed the heavy scatter-gun on a set of pegs driven into the cave wall. He passed a dirty hand down the other weapons that were racked from the floor to the low ceiling of the cave.

"You've got an arsenal there," commented Amy as she picked a bit of sharp rock from a bare heel. "You planning on a war?"

He turned slowly. "I collect," he said.

"Why so many?"

He scratched inside his filthy shirt and undershirt. "I am only one man," he replied, almost as though he was talking to himself. "Many men hunt me. Posses from Arizona, Nevada, California; Wells Fargo agents; Pinkerton men; Army. Many." He looked at the guns. He pointed to the top gun. "Winchester '73 in .44/40 caliber." He pointed to the others, each in turn. "Sharps Old Reliable in .50/70 Government; .45/70 issue Springfield; Winchester '76 in .45/75 caliber; Hopkins and Allen double-barreled twelve-gauge shotgun; Sharps .50/70 carbine." He opened an old ammunition box and held it out toward her. Half a dozen pistols were in it. "You know how I get all these fine guns?"

"I know how you got the last two," she quietly replied.

He grinned loosely. "All, I get like that."

The girl raised her head from where she lay exhausted on the floor. "You mean you *kill* men for them?" she asked.

"How else would I get them? But sometimes, like the driver, they have more than one gun."

"Thank God for small favors," said Amy drily.

"What does that mean?" he asked.

She looked quickly away from him. "Nothing."

He closed the box lid and picked up a cigar box. "Look," he said as he opened the lid.

"My God," said the girl. She covered her face with her hands.

There were at least six badges in the box, shining dully. "I collect these too," he said proudly.

"The same method?" asked Amy.

He nodded. "They come along with the guns," he said.

"Figures," said Amy. "Like marksmanship medals."

Queho nodded as he closed the box. He looked at the girl. "You, on the floor! You make beds!"

She sat up and looked at the haphazard pile of blankets and horseblankets, hides, and pelts lying at the side of the noisome cave. "There are no beds," she said.

"On floor! This ain't no hotel, missy!"

"How many beds?" she asked.

The other two women looked surreptitiously at the breed.

"How many you think we need?" he countered.

The army woman had lighted the fire. Smoke began to drift from the blackened, ash-choked fireplace. Queho leaped across the cave and kicked the smoldering wood out onto the cave floor. "Goddamn you, stupid woman!" he yelled. "You use dry wood! Squaw wood! You understand? Wood that not smoke! You want everyone within ten mile to see that goddamned smoke?"

She looked up at him, but did not answer. The answer was plain enough on her face.

He raised a fist, then lowered it. He laughed. "There ain't no one to see it out there anyway! Not today! Hotter than hell today! No water for anyone except river." He laughed a little wildly.

Amy watched the breed out of the corners of her eyes. There was something damned odd about his laugh. There wasn't any mirth in it. She had noticed it before, as she had noticed his changing moods. It was as though Queho drifted back and forth on the razor-edged line between sanity and insanity.

"How many beds?" quavered Lucille.

Queho was suddenly quiet. "Three," he replied.

"What about you?" she asked. She wasn't too bright.

He suddenly grinned. "Make mine twice as big as the others," he replied. "You maybe know why?"

No one answered him. In a little while he vanished around the bend in the cave just beyond the fireplace.

Lucille began to separate the bedding, now and again

turning her head away from the foul odors that emanated from the skins and pelts.

"Are you a virgin, Lucille?" suddenly asked Amy.

"I've been away to convent school," the girl replied primly.

"What does that have to do with it?" asked Mildred.

The girl was shocked. "Why, we *never* did things like *that!*"

"Your school was a lot different than mine then," said Mildred as she relighted the fire, this time with dry wood.

"Tell me the truth," persisted Amy.

The girl looked directly at Amy and shook her head. Maybe she wasn't lying after all.

Amy walked around the curve that led to the low mouth of the deep cave. Just below the overhanging roof of the cave mouth, Queho had dug down three feet to form a sort of wide trench. He had ramparted the outer side with natural-looking rocks, through which he had formed loop-holes that were now plugged with bits of rock. Amy stepped down into the trench and up onto the firestep at the base of the rampart. She looked behind herself and upward. Here the towering cliff above the cave beetled out, so that one standing on the cliff rim could not possibly look down and see the rampart or the cave mouth. To the right and left of the cave mouth, the cliff again bulged out smoothly, so that the cave could not be seen from either side and could not be approached from either flank. The only possible approach to the cave was directly below the rampart. Here lay a great slanted talus slope that baked and shimmered in the brazen sunlight. A fly could not crawl up that slope without being seen from the cave. The approach was also noisy. As Amy had experienced the night before when Queho had driven the three exhausted women up the slope and over the rampart into the cave. Nothing, except perhaps a gecko lizard or a hunting wildcat could come up that slope at night without creating one hell of a clashing racket of sliding, falling rock.

Below the talus slope was the *malpais* land, a broken and rebroken area created and then destroyed centuries past by cataclysmic upheavals and subsidences; a never-never land seemingly frozen in a tangle of writhing labyrinthine passages of sun-soaked rock baking in the intense heat and full of blind passages and thick-bodied rattlesnakes. Far below the cave, and beyond the *malpais* land, was the river—a silver, glistening arc of perhaps a mile or two in length buried at the bottom of a sheer-walled gorge. Somewhere upriver from that trap of a gorge was the place where Queho had ferried the three women, one at a time, across the dark, rushing river. Amy had not seen where he had hidden the boat. They had climbed to the rimrock before then.

"It is farther than it looks," said Queho from behind her.

She had been surprised, so quietly did he move, but she did not show it. "How long have you lived here?" she asked.

"Maybe three months. Not sure."

"Alone?"

"Always. One time, long ago, I lived here too."

"Why did you take us from the coach?"

"Maybe I needed woman—a *squaw*, maybe."

"Yes, but *three* of us. . . ."

"I only knew of one woman on coach."

"The army woman."

"Yes."

She turned and looked up into his strange, brooding face. "How did you know she would be on that coach?"

He looked down the heat-shimmering talus slope and across the *malpais* land to the distant river. "It is enough for you that I *did* know," he replied after a time.

"You hate her."

His strong, dirty hands came together with force and worked one against the other, so that the veins stood out on their backs like writhing worms beneath the dark skin. His breathing came hard and fast.

"You could have killed her for your revenge, whatever it is."

"She had me sent to hell! I take her into a hell I choose now! She lie! She cheat! She bad all through! No good! No good."

Amy wisely shifted the subject. "The girl has not known a man," she said.

"How you know?"

"She told me."

Queho laughed. "Women fools. They believe only what they want to."

"And men do not?"

He searched her rather plain-looking face.

"Will you let her alone?" asked Amy.

"I boss here! You women do what Queho says you do!"

"That's not an answer," said Amy bravely.

"I won't take her tonight," he said. "If someone take her place," he added quickly, as an afterthought.

The smell of the breed almost sickened her. "I'll take her place," she volunteered.

He looked back at the cave. "The other one."

"She won't come to you, Queho."

He looked down at his powerful hands, greasy, dirty-tipped, with ragged broken nails. "She'll come. On her fat knees! Crawling to me! She'll come to me! You understand! Like *squaw!*"

"She never will."

His eyes held hers. She could not look into them, yet she could not turn away from them, and what she saw, or thought she saw, frightened her. He suddenly looked over her head, as though something else had crossed his confused mind. "I'll wait," he promised.

"I'll come to you tonight if you leave the girl alone."

He grinned suddenly. *"Enju!* But I won't be here tonight. Got to hunt. Three squaws eat too much. Need more food."

"What kind of game do you hunt in this country of hell?"

"My kind of game," he quietly replied. "You'll see." He walked into the cave.

Amy came into the cave a few minutes after Queho. He was gone and so was the Winchester '73. Queho was gone, but he had left his peculiar scent behind—a compound of stale sweat, urine, rancid grease, and foul clothing. It was not as unpleasant as it had been, thought Amy. Maybe she was getting used to it. "My God," she said at the thought.

Mildred looked up from her pallet. *"He's* not around here. What does that mean?"

"I think I'm getting used to his stink."

The three of them sat there as darkness filled the cave. After a time, Amy found a candle and lighted it. She walked toward the rear of the cave.

"Where are you going?" asked Mildred.

"Exploring. There must be another way out of here."

"It's dark, Amy," said Lucille fearfully. "He said we were not to make a light after dusk, for fear it would be seen from the outside."

"The light can't be seen from back here!" called Amy.

"Are you sure he's gone?"

Amy shrugged. "I'll risk it."

The seemingly solid rock of the heights was internally rotten, honeycombed with a bewildering lacework of labyrinthine passages pitted with deep holes that seemed bottomless. Three times Amy walked up blind passageways and once into a natural room that stank like an abattoir with a miasma of garbage, offal, and human waste left there by Queho. One of the passageways ended against a wall with a deep pit below it. Amy dropped stones into it and strained her ears, only to hear the stones strike deep, deep below in the stygian darkness. Once she thought she heard someone laughing in the darkness, but there was no one there—at least she *thought* no one was there.

Amy plodded back to the outer cave and found tobacco and papers. She expertly shaped a cigarette, lighted it from the candle, then blew out the candle.

"Well?" asked Mildred.

Amy drew on the cigarette, lighting her thoughtful face. "Forget it," she said. "Queho is the only person who knows the way out of there."

"Will he be back tonight?" asked Lucille anxiously.

"You'll be safe, honey," promised Amy.

"How do you know?"

"He told me."

"He seems to tell you a lot of things," slyly suggested Mildred. She shaped a cigarette in the darkness.

"Not being able to talk to men has never been one of my failings. I've found it too damned easy to talk with them."

"He's not a man! He's a rapist! A breed! A killer!"

"Have you ever wondered why?"

Mildred lighted up. "That's an excuse?"

"Born on the wrong side of the blanket. The catch-colt bastard son of a Mohave Apache squaw, who was herself a half-breed Mexican, and a man who was half black and half white, a mulatto, if you will, serving with black men."

"He was a nigger! A Buffalo Soldier!"

"I've heard they are damned good soldiers."

"Where did you hear that?"

Amy blew a smoke ring. "I've known a few army men in my time."

"Blacks?"

Amy looked at her through the darkness. "No," she denied quietly.

"You've sunk so low in your sex that some day even the nigger troopers won't want you!"

Amy smiled a little. "Come to think of it, Queho got into your lacy drawers down at Fort Mohave. How was it, sister?"

"Damn you! That was *rape!*"

Amy laughed. "You didn't answer my question."

"Well, anyway, if he does want a woman, he can have Lucy there."

"Maybe Amy will go with him," suggested Lucille.

"Maybe he won't want to risk a dose from her. You know what I mean, honey?" Mildred laughed. "It isn't so bad the first time a man takes you, honey. It hurts, but after a few more times, it's all right."

"But not here!"

"What are you saving it for?" Mildred grinned in the darkness. "I know! For your future husband! Is that it?"

"Of course I am! Didn't you?"

Mildred laughed. "It's not exactly the time for confession, honey."

Amy snubbed out her cigarette. "I'm beat," she said. "We might as well get some sleep tonight. Tomorrow night might be different."

They lay down on their pallets. Queho was gone in the flesh, but something of him lingered on in the cave. It was more than the animal odor he left—it was a brooding, haunting fear of the man himself.

THIRTEEN

THERE WAS A spring of cold, clear water that fed a wide and shallow pool that was set like a green jewel at the far end of a multi-colored canyon, wearing a fringe of willows and alders. The water was always cold and pure, even when the summer sun was blasting the empty desert beyond the down-sloping floor of the lower part of the high-walled canyon. During the day, there was the constant droning of insects mingled with the soft whispering of the dry wind gently swaying the leaves and allowing the sunlight to strike through the overhanging arch of the trees to glisten on the dappled water. Leaves that had dried and fallen into the pool would drift like small, curled canoes to form a golden, intermittently sunlighted mass floating at the upper end of the pool. When the sun shone fully on the mass, like a field of goldenrod, a man might dream of the gold he could not find in the mountains and desert beyond the magic of the canyon.

During the day, the canyon wrens twittered in the trees, and just before sunset, the cliff swallows would swoop down for flying insects. After sundown, in the shadowed dusk, the velvet winged bats would come from the openings in the cliff and fly in a mounting line like scraps of charred paper impelled by the night wind. In the soft darkness before the coming of the moonlight, there would be quiet splashings beside the pool, alternating with moments of utter silence as the shy nocturnal creatures drank and then listened to the night. Sometimes in the clear moonlight the deer would raise their dripping muzzles from the water to listen for the soft footed approach of the great old cougar who lived alone in the deeper reaches of the canyon.

It was a lonely place, yet a man was never alone there. The sun would shine though the gaps in the leaves to form a dappled, constantly moving rhythmic pattern on the surface of the pool that was almost like a silent kind of music—soul music.

Boot-soles scuffled on hard rock. Metal grated against metal. A heavy door was pushed gratingly open on long, unoiled hinges to bang back against a wall of solid living rock. Then it was quiet again, except for the heavy sound of breathing in the darkness. As the eyes became accustomed to it, there was the faint rectangle of the opened door, dark gray limned against the deep darkness of the natural rock cell.

Something scratched. A tiny bulb of flame spurted into fiery life at the tip of a match that was slowly raised to reveal a pair of eyes that glittered in the flame light. The eyes steadied on the dim figure of a man seated on the rock floor with his back against the wall and with his legs outthrust. A pair of iron cuffs ringed his bare, festering ankles, and between his ankles there was a heavy bar of stout strap-iron. From the iron bar there extended a heavy chain padlocked into a great rusted iron ring, whose hasp was sunk deeply into the rock floor.

"How are you, Kershaw?" asked the man with the match.

"I'll survive, warden," drily replied Lee Kershaw.

"I've often wondered how."

Lee closed his eyes. The dreamlike vision of the magic canyon and the charmed pool seemed to come back to him. "You wouldn't understand," he said. The warden closed the door and then lighted a candle. He placed it on the floor. "How long have you been in darkness?" he asked.

"One can't tell time in here."

"It was a week, Kershaw."

"If you knew, why did you ask? What do you want from me?"

"Maybe I came to see how you were."

Kershaw laughed. It was a rich and solid laugh; certainly not the cackling, dry-stick laughter of a man who had just spent a week as punishment for an infraction of the rules in total darkness in the notorious Snake Den of Yuma Pen during the very core of the summer heat.

"Few men can keep their sanity in here, Kershaw."

"Their name is not Kershaw."

The candle guttered a little, casting alternate patches of light on the thickly spider-webbed walls, only to shift them back into thick darkness again to seek another place to light.

"How much longer do you have to serve, Kershaw?"

"Nineteen years and a few months, I think."

"Nineteen and a half, to be exact. Understand that I want to impress that on your mind."

"It *has* been impressed on my mind, sir. I was judged by a jury of my peers, and sentenced by the toughest hanging judge in the Territory, influenced somewhat, no doubt, by the Governor of the Territory, who was, in turn, influenced by his esteemed friend Kentucky Colonel Will Felding, of the Indian Bureau."

"It could have been worse. Murder is a hanging offense."

"Hanging might have been the better choice over this place."

"Hell is tougher than Yuma Pen."

"If one has been to Yuma Pen, he *has* been to hell."

"You'll never last nineteen and a half years in here."

"I'll try."

The warden shook his head. He squatted on his heels and took out the makings. He shaped a cigarette and placed it between Lee's bearded lips. He thumb-snapped a match into flame and lighted the cigarette. *"Gracias,"* murmured Lee, always the gentleman. *"Por nada,"* responded the warden. He fashioned a cigarette for himself and lighted it. He looked at Lee over the flare of the match. "Tell me, Kershaw, just between you and me—were you really innocent?"

"Every man between these walls will tell you that he is innocent. You didn't come here to ask me that. What difference can it possibly make now?"

"Because I can give you a chance to wipe out that nineteen and a half years you will not live to serve out. I'd like to know I helped an innocent man."

Lee Kershaw looked at his cigarette as though he had never seen one before. "Leave the makings," he suggested. "Close the door from the outside, please, and take the candle with you. I think better in the darkness."

The warden stood up with the candle in his hand. "You may be able to fool those stupid, illiterate cons out there in the yard, Kershaw, but you can't fool me. You're holding on to your reason with all the strength and willpower you have, which is considerable, I must admit, but it will not be enough, Kershaw! Right now you are gambling first with your reason and then you will gamble with your very life, and you will lose! Outside these walls, men like you are well-nigh invincible, but you crack like a rotten egg in here, as easily as those more stupid cons outside will do. The hell of it, Kershaw, is that you know I'm right!"

"You've been reading books again, warden."

"Once you are broken, there will be no going back."

"Hear, hear," Lee jibed softly.

The warden blew out the candle. "I'm going to walk to that door, Kershaw. I'm going to open it. Just call out to me before I close that door, Kershaw, because, before God, if you do not call out to me, you'll never again have a chance to leave Yuma Pen alive."

The Snake Den was as black as the anteroom to hell itself. Lee Kershaw heard the heavy breathing of the big man who stood there in the darkness looking down at him. The reek of the greasy candle hung in the stale, stifling air.

Sweat leaked from Lee Kershaw's body and ran itching down his sides. He closed his eyes.

Leather boots scuffed on rock. One step. . . . *The cliff swallows always darted swiftly about until dusk.* Two steps. . . . *When the sun was gone and the dusk came, the silent bats would come forth to relieve the guard of cliff swallows.* Three steps. . . . *It would be a little while yet before the velvet-footed coyotes came up from the desert to drink.* Four steps. . . . The doorhandle was turned, and a faint streak of grayish light showed between it and the wall. Before God! *What had happened to the spring?* There was nothing in the canyon now but utter darkness, like the darkness of the Snake Den, broken only by a faint and widening bar of gray light. The door hinges creaked. There was a moment's hesitation. The hinges creaked again, and the gap of gray began to narrow.

"Wait!" called out Lee.

The key soon clicked in the lock of the leg-irons.

FOURTEEN

THE WARDEN CLOSED the door behind himself and Lee Kershaw. "Here is your man, gentlemen," he said.

"Will he go?" asked a familiar voice.

Lee looked across the shaded living room of the warden's quarters into the face of Colonel Will Felding. Beside the agent sat a little wizened man wearing pince-nez glasses, who looked steadily at Lee like a bright-eyed little bird.

"Uriah Heep," observed Lee.

"I beg your pardon?" said the little birdlike man.

"This gentleman is Marcus Wrenn," explained the warden. "He is secretary to the governor."

"Uriah Heep," repeated Lee.

"Is he all right, warden?" asked Wrenn.

"He's all wrong," said the warden.

The merry tinkling of ice against the sides of a glass pitcher forecasted the arrival of Sarah, the warden's wife, bearing a tray with a pitcher of pink lemonade and three tall glasses. She served the three men.

"Make mine a beer, ma'am," suggested Lee from where he sat on the floor with his back against the wall.

"Of all the nerve!" cried Sarah.

"Get him a couple of bottles, Sarah," said the warden.

"Have you told him, Henry?" asked Felding of the warden.

"Only that he has a chance of wiping out his sentence."

"What about it, Mister Kershaw?" asked Wrenn.

Lee's gray eyes were on the two bottles of beer being

brought into the room by Sarah. They were tall and mistysided. Lee's throat went thoroughly dry and speechless. He gripped a bottle and twisted off the wire. The cap popped. The cold beer foamed and gurgled down Lee's throat. He lowered the bottle half-emptied. "Mother's own milk!" he gasped.

"I asked you a question," reminded Wrenn.

"You're representing the governor?" asked Lee.

Wrenn nodded.

Lee looked at Felding. "What's your part in the deal?"

"My wife, whom you will remember, Kershaw."

"You honor me," said Lee drily.

"Tell him, gentlemen," suggested the warden. "How's the beer, Kershaw?"

"Prime, warden," replied Lee as he raised the bottle.

"It's about Queho," stated Felding.

Lee looked slowly up at him. "He's alive?"

"That is correct."

"*Where?*" softly asked Lee. A powerful hand tightened about the neck of the beer bottle.

"Up north, somewhere along the Colorado River, perhaps in Arizona, Nevada, or even California. We don't know for sure."

"You're sure? I mean—that he's *alive?*"

"We're positive."

The bottle snapped in the crush of Lee's hand. Beer and blood intermingled and ran down to soak into his convict's striped trousers.

Sarah came bustling in to treat and bandage Lee's wound. She cleaned up the mess and brought Lee another beer. The warden tossed the makings to Lee.

"What is it you want from me?" asked Lee as he shaped a quirly.

"We want you to go in and get Queho," replied Felding.

"No man can do that," replied Lee.

"You can," said the warden.

"Only you," added Wrenn. "They say no man knows that country better than you do."

"That is not so," corrected Lee as he lighted up. "Queho does. What brought all this on?"

The three of them told him, each of them taking a part, as in the chorus in a Greek tragedy, until the bloody tale was finished.

Lee grinned wryly as he opened the beer bottle. "You've got to give him credit. Who else could have gotten away with it?"

"*You*, maybe," replied Felding.

Lee shook his head. "There would have been no incentive for me. I do not want your wife, Colonel. I never did. If I had escaped with Queho, instead of being quickly recaptured, I would have been in Mexico these past months, hiding out from the *Rurales*, of course, but safe from Arizona law." He shrugged. "But Queho thinks differently."

"Why?" asked Wrenn.

Lee looked up at him. "Because he is not a man of our society. The Indians never fully accepted him because he has the blood of black and white in him. The blacks will not accept him because he has the blood of Indian and white man in him. The Mexicans will not accept him because he has mixed gringo blood, and they are superstitious about the blacks. In short, gentlemen he is Ishmael. No! More! He is a pariah; a social leper!"

"Yet you seemed to have accepted him," suggested the warden.

Lee smiled crookedly. "I had no choice. He once saved my life. I could depend upon him. Later, we were cellmates for months. I killed time by trying to teach him. I thought I had grown to know him."

"I meant more than that, Kershaw. You went to prison partly because of him."

Lee looked into Felding's eyes and the agent turned away.

"No man can accept Queho'," murmured Lee. "*No man. . . .*"

"And yet, without you, he could not have escaped from Yuma Pen."

"We were supposed to have helped each other," said Lee drily.

"But, when the time came for Queho to make his choice, to keep on to freedom, or to turn back and help you, risking recapture, he abandoned you, the man who had helped him to escape, and he left you to the mercy of the Cocopah trackers."

Lee nodded. "They would have killed him, after torture, rather than bring him in alive, or perhaps *half* alive, as they did me, for their fifty dollars reward." The big, dirty hands closed tightly on the beer bottle. "I haven't forgotten that," he softly added.

"Some say," persisted the warden, "that the choice was yours—to escape yourself and leave Queho to the trackers, or to stay behind to lead the trackers astray so that he might escape, knowing all the time that you could not escape."

"Of such things are legends woven," said Lee quietly.

"Then you must bear no love for Queho," said Wrenn.

Lee smiled faintly. "Revenge is bitter fruit, gentlemen." His bearded face changed into an enigmatic mask. "Let's get down to business, gentlemen. Your deal? *Offer*, I should say."

Felding and the warden looked at Wrenn. He adjusted his pince-nez and cleared his scrawny throat. "If you will go in after Queho and rescue the two women he has kidnapped, the governor will grant you a full pardon."

"What's to prevent me from taking off for Mexico once I'm out from behind these walls?"

"Your word."

"You'll take that?"

"You are known to be a man of your word."

Lee slowly began to shape a cigarette. "A failing, in this

mercenary world. And what of Queho? Do you want him too?"

It was very quiet in the shade-darkened room.

"You know I will have to kill him to succeed," added Lee.

No one spoke.

Lee lighted up. "Or *he* will have to kill *me*. There can be no other way between us, gentlemen."

"We knew that," said Felding.

"The most dangerous game in the world," continued Lee, almost as though he was talking to himself. "Man hunting man."

"Who is better at that game than you are, Kershaw?" reminded the warden. "Or once *were*," he hastily corrected himself.

"Maybe Queho," quietly replied Lee, "although perhaps he doesn't know it himself yet. And, he will be playing on his own field, a distinct advantage at any time, with the odds being even if we are on more or less neutral ground."

"You talk like a professional," put in Wrenn.

"I *am* a professional."

"Well?" asked Wrenn. "What is your decision?"

Lee closed his eyes. The memory of the cool, shaded upper canyon with its spring would not come back to him. Instead, he saw nothing but the shifting, mind-cracking darkness of the Snake Den.

"Nineteen more years, Kershaw," reminded the warden.

"Nineteen and a half," corrected Lee. "When do I get the pardon?" He opened his eyes.

"Upon the delivery of the two women," said Felding.

"And the head of Queho in a sack? It will stink in the furnace heat."

"That will not be necessary," primly replied Wrenn.

Lee looked at the fat, sweating porcine face of Felding. "The Colonel, there, might want another tobacco jar," he murmured.

"I do not understand," said Wrenn.

"No matter, sir," said Lee.

"We will take your word on the death of Queho," promised Wrenn.

"Most kind,"murmured Lee.

"Will you go then?" asked Felding.

"All right," agreed Lee.

He stood up. "I'll need expense money. A bath, fresh clothing, guns, a horse, and passage upriver to Fort Mohave for myself and the horse. I place first priority on the bath."

Wrenn nodded. He placed five crisp hundred dollar bills on the marble-topped table. "Is that enough?" he asked.

"For starters. Do you want a receipt?"

Wrenn shook his head. "No records are to be kept of this transaction."

Felding stood up and took his hat. "I hope that you still do not harbor any ill will against my wife or myself for the charges placed against you by us at Fort Mohave."

"Little things like attempted rape, assault, and second-degree murder? No gentleman would hold such things against the character of a lady such as Mrs. Felding, sir, and yourself, of course, Colonel."

"You honor my wife and myself, sir!"

The warden looked searchingly at the bearded face of Lee Kershaw. He'd never be able to figure out the man.

"All I want to do," added Lee, "is to get my hairy old ass out of Yuma Pen, sir! I'd go into that country of hellfire to bring out Lucretia Borgia, if you had promised me a pardon for that."

"I do not care for that comparison, sir," protested Felding.

Lee shrugged. "I do not have to like your wife, sir, to try and save her life. I would do the same for any woman in such a situation."

"Good luck then," said Wrenn. He opened the door and let in a blast of heat and sunlight. Felding walked past him.

"One moment!" called out Lee.

They turned and looked quizzically at him.

"You mentioned that *three* women had been taken by Queho. Yet you have mentioned only two of them, referring to Mrs. Felding and Lucille Winston, the governor's niece. What about the third woman. Who is she?"

"She's nothing," replied Wrenn.

"Only a whore," added Felding.

"I see," said Lee quietly. "Only a whore. Nothing. . . ." They closed the door behind themselves.

FIFTEEN

THE COPA DE Oro Mine was situated high on the barren slopes overlooking the lower mountain spurs and the flat desert below them. Across the desert was the distant north-south road, and at right angles to that road was the branch road, a single, deeply rutted track that came straight as a bowstring across the desert toward the mountains until it reached the lower slopes, where it then vanished from the sight of anyone up at the mine by passing around behind a pinnacled rock formation, only to reappear at the eastern side of the formation to slant transversely up a treacherous road cut into the mountainside to ascend to the mine. It was a bad road to travel in full daylight, and at night it was virtually impossible to ascend.

A man watching the road from the mine could see all the way across the desert to the faintly distinguishable line of the north-south road until it turned behind the pinnacles. Thus, anything moving on either road could be seen because of the rising dust, at least during the daylight hours or on bright, moonlit nights. In the days of the Paiute troubles, a watchman was always kept on the heights above the mine to watch the roads. He wasn't up there to look for Paiutes, because they were never seen unless they wanted to be seen. He was there to watch for the rising dust that would forecast the coming of the vital freight-wagons delivering supplies to the mine. When dust arose on the branch road, it would then be time to send out an armed escort of mine employees to guard the freight wagons until they reached the mine. The ore wagons leaving the mine were never guarded, for a Paiute had little use for the white man's madness of gold. But the contents of the freight wagons were treasure indeed for the Paiutes.

For several years, since the Paiutes had been quiet and the Mohave Apaches had stayed, reservation bound, far to the south, it had not been necessary to keep a watchman on the heights. Now that Queho was haunting the empty land, coming and going in the infernal temperatures like a disembodied spirit, a watchman was again kept on the heights, softly cursing his fate. He sat under a square of worn and patched wagon canvas armed with a rifle and a pair of powerful field glasses, trying to keep awake.

This day, the dust moved along the north-south road until it reached the junction of the branch road in the late afternoon. Then the dust changed direction and moved slowly toward the east along the branch road. The sun was already slanting low to the west. The wagons were hours late. They would not be driven up the steep mountain road until daylight, therefore they would stop, by custom, beyond the pinnacles from dusk to dawn, out of sight of anyone up at the Copa de Oro.

The watchman this day picked up a melon-sized rock and dropped it. It struck the galvanized iron roof of the mine office far below and sent a dull resounding echo against the mountain flank. Melvin Lusk, the mine manager, came out of the office and looked up at the watchman.

"Dust on the road, Mister Lusk!" yelled the watchman. "It'll be the freight wagons!"

Lusk shaded his eyes and looked toward the dust. The wagons would not be driven up to the mine before daylight. He was shorthanded at the mine as it was. Even Queho would think twice before he jumped three tough teamsters armed and usually spoiling for a fight.

"Can I come down now?" called the watchman.

Lusk waved the man down. He went back into his office and closed the door.

The watchman reached the mine buildings just as the sun went down beyond the mountains.

The lead freight wagon ground to a dusty halt behind the pinnacles. The lead teamster clambered down to the ground and eased his crotch. He walked back to the other wagons. "We'll stay here tonight and go up at dawn," he said.

The three teamsters walked to the water barrel lashed onto the side of the first wagon. It was then that they saw the lean, moccasined man step silently out of the shadows of the pinnacles and slowly raise his cocked Winchester '73.

There was no moon that night. About midnight, three rapid-fire shots ripped out and echoed flatly against the pinnacles, rebounding to roll out across the darkened desert and then die away. No one heard the shooting up at the mine.

The sun came up behind the mountains and lighted the desert, warming the eastern face of the pinnacles. No dust arose from behind the pinnacles.

Manager Lusk shoved back his plate and drained his coffee cup. He lighted a cigar and stood up. "Joe," he said to the watchman, "go down and see what's holding up the wagons."

Joe rode slowly down the winding mountain road. The sun was already hot on his back. No smoke rose from a morning campfire beyond the pinnacles. Joe rounded the pinnacles. The three wagons stood in a line with their knife-slashed tilts flapping idly in the morning breeze. The twelve mules were nowhere in sight.

"Anybody here?" yelled Joe.

"Anybody here? Anybody here? Anybody here?" echoed the pinnacles.

There was no reply.

The roan shied and blew as Joe rode around the pinnacles. The three teamsters lay sprawled on the ground.

Early-rising flies were already swarming about the shattered messes soft-nosed 200-grain .44/40 bullets can make out of the backs of skulls when fired at short range.

The wagons had been carefully looted. A wide track of mule-hoofs showed on the harsh desert soil, vanishing into the northern distance.

SIXTEEN

"IT CAN'T BE more than a mile down to the river," insisted Amy.

"As the crow flies," argued Mildred. "Look! Those rocks down there are all up and down like teeth on a saw."

"There has to be a way! He must get his water from the river down there and I'll bet *he* doesn't climb over those rocks to get it. There must be a way through them."

"And what happens if we do get to the river?"

"We can follow it downstream until we find a mine or a ranch or something."

"I don't quite think we can walk along beside the river like we would on a pathway through a park."

"Maybe we can swim across."

Mildred laughed. "You'll end up miles downstream rolling along the bottom."

"He's been gone three days," said the girl. "Maybe he won't be back. Maybe he's dead or captured. There's no food left, and hardly any water."

Mildred eyed the girl. "You sound almost sorry that something might have happened to him."

Lucille looked up a little dreamily. "He hasn't been unkind to *me*. But I think he'll be back. They can't capture or kill *him*."

Amy eyed her curiously. "What's all this?" she asked.

"Hero worship," said Mildred drily. "He's probably the first man who's ever looked twice at her."

"He escaped from Yuma Pen," continued the girl,

almost as though she was talking to herself. She looked up brightly. "Have you ever heard of anyone doing *that?*"

Amy peered over the rampart. The heat waves rose from the baking talus slope and distorted the *malpais* land and the crescent of river beyond it. "There has to be a way through there!"

"It will be like a furnace down there," argued Mildred. "And the snakes! It will be alive with them!"

"They won't come out into the sun. It would kill them. We'll just have to watch where we step and where we put our hands."

Amy filled three canteens with the last of the water. "We can't stay here any longer, no matter how much you argue. If he doesn't come back by tomorrow, we'll die of thirst in here."

"Leave my water here," said Lucille. "I'm not going."

Amy handed her a canteen. "Get up," she ordered. "We haven't much time left to get down there before dark."

Lucille shook her head. "I'm staying."

Amy dragged her to her feet. "Come on," she ordered.

Mildred shook her head. "You won't get her to go that way, sister." She snatched Lucille's canteen away from her. "If you want to catch a rabbit like this one here, you've got to lure her with a carrot—in this case, the last of the water."

Amy took the Hopkins and Allen shotgun from the rack. She broke it to check the loads, then briskly snapped it shut.

"What do you intend doing with that?" asked the girl. "You wouldn't shoot him with it, would you?"

Amy clambered to the top of the rampart. "Try me," she cheerily replied. She dropped out of sight on the far side of the rampart.

Amy stopped at the foot of the talus slope. "Look," she said.

They looked up toward the cave. There was no indication whatsoever of the cave or of the rampart in front of it, so skillfully had Queho used natural materials to blend in his work with the surrounding features.

Amy walked into the labyrinth of the *malpais*.

An hour later, the three women staggered out of the natural baking oven, streaming with sweat and gasping for breath in the stifling, heated air. Their canteens were half empty.

"I'm going back," gasped Lucille.

"Where?" asked Amy.

Nowhere could they see the way they had come, or any feature that might identify the approach of the hidden cave.

"Come on," said Amy. She started back toward the *malpais*. Mildred followed her.

The girl stood there in the burning sunlight, staring up the slopes with burning eyes. She suddenly realized that Amy was right. She turned. "Wait!" she cried. The two women were out of sight. Lucille ran after them, right into the winding labyrinth from which they had just come.

The sun was low in the west. The two canteens were empty. "I knew we'd never make it! Damn you anyway!" snapped Mildred.

"I'm not licked yet!"

"The light is almost gone."

"We can wait until the dawn."

Queho found them sitting silently in the darkness. They were less than two hundred yards from the hidden way by which he reached the river for his water. He picked up the shotgun and jerked his head toward the heights, shadowed in darkness. He did not look back as he led the way. They stumbled and gasped behind him like two frightened little girls who had run away from home and had been overtaken by the hostile darkness.

Lucille was seated by the fireplace contentedly stirring a stew. She did not look up as the two women staggered into the cave. "Smells delicious," Amy observed drily. "What is it?"

"Stew! I made it myself!"

"Out of aged mule-meat?" asked Mildred.

Lucille shook her head. "Corned beef and dessicated vegetables."

"Where did you get it?" asked Amy.

Lucille pointed with her dripping spoon at a pile of boxes stacked against the wall. Blackly stamped on the yellow pinewood were the bold letters—COPA DE ORO MINE.

SEVENTEEN

"GODDAMNIT!" ROARED SHERIFF Jim Hathaway. He smashed a meaty fist down atop the map he had spread on a flat rock. "How in God's name Queho can vanish into thin air with twelve mules and about a wagonload of supplies is beyond me!"

No one spoke. The possemen quietly smoked, watching the red-faced sheriff out of the corners of their sun-reddened eyes. The darkness of the desert persistently crept in about the wavering, shifting circle of firelight until someone threw more brush on the fire. A big coffeepot bubbled at the edge of the embers.

One of the men coughed, and the others looked accusingly at him. Then their eyes slanted outward into the soft darkness of the desert night. It was as though someone, or *something*, was watching them from the very edge of the firelight. The Paiute trackers were back in the shadows of the rocks, squatting on their heels, arms resting on their muscular thighs, lean and dirty hands hanging limply down. They could have told Hathaway that only Queho could hold up three freight wagons, kill three strong, armed men, and drive twelve mules off into the darkness laden with fine loot, only to vanish into thin air. The crazy white men still persisted in thinking they were dealing with a *man*.

"The Paiutes lost the trail three miles this side of the river, Jim," said the deputy sheriff.

"They'd lose their goddamned skinny asses if they didn't hold onto them with both hands!" roared the sheriff.

Dan looked toward the shadowed Paiutes. He could see the firelight reflecting moistly from their eyes. "It ain't that, Jim. They might have been able to track him right to the river but they didn't want to and nothing on God's earth can make them do that."

The fire died low. The thick bed of ashes peeped out a secretive ruby-red eye now and then, or a short-lived dancing sprout of flame. The flame would cast an eerie light on the tired faces of the possemen, only to die down and then reappear at another place in the wide bed of ashes.

Not even the Paiutes heard the lone man ghost silently through the darkness on moccasined feet. One minute he was not there, and the next minute he was there. His appearance was so unexpected that no one moved at first. Then the Paiutes, as one man, vanished back in among the rocks, to run silently through the darkness they feared almost as much as they feared Queho.

A Winchester action was quickly worked. The possemen stood up with their rifles in their hands.

"Who're you, mister?" demanded the sheriff.

"The name is Kershaw." Lee walked noiselessly to the fire. He filled a cup with the steaming, powerful brew. "You might as well turn back tomorrow morning," he suggested. "Queho will not be on this side of the river now. It's raining in the mountains to the east. The river is rising. You'll have the hell of a time getting across it, if you had that in mind."

"We did. You got here fast, Kershaw."

"Took the *Cocopah* upriver until it ran out of water. They're waiting for enough water to get upriver to Callville. I backtracked to find you here."

"How did you know where to find us?" asked the lawman stupidly.

Lee spat into the fire to raise a tiny spurt of steam. "A blind man could have seen your fire ten miles from here at dusk. I could hear you talking half a mile from here when the wind shifted."

The possemen surreptitiously studied the lean, bearded face of the man Lee Kershaw. Most of them knew him only by reputation. They knew he had been the man who had once traced down the Paiute murderer Ahvote and had brought him back to Prescott to await his execution. They knew, too, that if it had not been for Queho, Ahvote might have killed Kershaw. He was known as the best scout and manhunter in the Southwest and in Northern Mexico as well. That is, until he was put behind the bars at Yuma Pen. He was uncanny with a rifle (his seven-hundred-yard shot to hit and kill Ahvote was already legend); he was a lightning-fast draw with the six-gun; he was a man who could fight equally well under the Marquess of Queensberry rules, or with knife, fist, and boot. Strangest of all, he was self-educated and, incredibly, he even read books! His short service with Queho as his partner had established them as the best scouting-and-tracking pair in the business, with the odds being even as to which of the two of them was the better, and few takers on either one of them.

"Queho had a two day start this time," complained Hathaway. "The Paiutes lost his trail some miles on this side of the river."

"That figures." Lee smiled. "At least that's what they told you, Hathaway. They don't *want* to find him."

"And you can find him?"

"I'll take a look, Sheriff."

"You aim to hunt him alone?" asked Dan.

Lee nodded.

"I can send some of the boys with you," offered Hathaway.

The "boys" looked uneasily at each other.

"To help look for Queho or to keep an eye on me, Sheriff?" asked Lee. "The way you hunt for Queho, it's a wonder you get near him at all."

"You can do better?" asked Dan.

"I can," admitted Lee. He looked out into the soft desert darkness beyond the faint firelight. "He might very well be out there right now watching us."

"If he was," said Hathaway wisely, "you wouldn't be standing beside that fire like a clay pigeon."

Some months after Queho and Kershaw had been placed in Yuma Pen, they had made a well-planned break for freedom. Trouble was, they might have *planned* a double break, but *only* Queho had made it to freedom. Some said Queho had sacrificed Kershaw to make his escape; others said Kershaw had sacrificed himself to let Queho escape. Only two living men knew the answer to that one—Kershaw and Queho. Kershaw had never talked about it after his recapture, and Queho hadn't exactly stuck around publicly to give his version of the affair.

"Is there any help I can give you at all?" asked Hathaway.

"They told me you'd swear me in as a special deputy with a warrant for Queho. You know, like a hunting license." Lee grinned like a hungry lobo. "Besides, it will protect me from anyone who might mistakenly think I'm on the run from Yuma Pen."

"And what's to protect you from Queho?" drily asked Dan.

Lee shrugged. "In the game we will play, the first one of us who sees the other will likely win."

Hathaway took out a deputy badge and a warrant. "Hold up your right hand," he said. "Without the damned coffee cup in it!" He duly swore in Lee and gave him the warrant. "We've made a deal with California and Nevada. The badge and the warrant are as good in their territory as they are here in Arizona."

"They say Queho collects the guns and badges of the men who hunt him, Kershaw," needled Dan. "You know—like trophies."

"How many so far?"

"God alone really knows. Couple of deputies, a mine watchman, three teamsters. A Nevada deputy went missing two months ago. A Wells Fargo man went in after Queho and hasn't been seen since. Some say he has killed twelve men since he got out of Yuma. That would make you unlucky thirteen, Kershaw."

Lee looked at him. "Seems to me that *all* of them were unlucky, mister."

"Nevada is keeping a posse in the field at all times," hastily interposed Hathaway. "There are now two operating from Arizona and one from California. The Army is preparing to send in a strong patrol. There's little chance of him ever getting out of that hell's area where he's holed up."

Lee looked off into the darkness toward the unseen river. "He won't attempt a break," he quietly prophesied. "He'd condemned himself to a prison just the same as the one he broke out of, except that it's bigger, and a hell of a lot lonelier. Bigger, perhaps, but just as confining."

"You sound like you're almost sorry for him," accused Dan.

"There's no place for him in our society. The whites, blacks, Indians, and the breeds don't want him. No matter where he goes, he's already condemned. No matter where he tries to go, the law is hunting for him. Dead or alive, mister, with the emphasis on *dead*. He has literally condemned himself to life imprisonment in the barren mountains and lost canyons along the Colorado River."

Hathaway nodded. "With twelve mule-loads of supplies. He has an inexhaustible supply of water from the river. He has innumerable hideouts known only to himself, and has an armory of rifles, shotguns, and pistols, and plenty of ammunition for all of them."

"Coupled with the hunting-and-killing instincts of a predatory animal," added Lee. "He's king in those canyons, gentlemen, and don't you ever forget it."

It was very quiet again.

A horse whinnied out of the darkness.

Men grabbed for their rifles.

"Mine," said Lee.

When the fire had died down to a thick bed of ashes, Lee vanished into the darkness as quickly and as silently as he had appeared.

EIGHTEEN

THE DAWN LIGHT had crept into the river gorge an hour before and had slowly erased the deep shadows. The light grew. There was no wind. Nothing moved except the river, which now flowed swiftly and higher because of the rains in the mountains far to the east.

The faint mule-tracks had ended a mile from the river at the edge of an exposed rock-shield on the lower ground on the Arizona side of the river. Lee Kershaw squatted behind a rock outcropping that concealed him from anyone who might be watching the gorge from the almost sheer heights across the river. Behind Lee was a broken land; a mad helter-skelter of distorted and shattered rock virtually impossible for mules and horses to pass through; yet, somehow Queho must have gotten his loot-laden mules to the river and *across* the river. That was the puzzle.

Lee studied the upriver shore. There the rock shield slanted down under the surface, and just northeast of it there was a wide, gravelly beach.

Lee worked his way through the *malpais* land behind the rock shield. Here he found his first clue. It was a heavy stone, shaped like a great pear, whose heavier and darker side lay upward, indicating that some force had struck it and turned it over, and recently, for the sun had not yet had time to lighten the darker surface. A man's foot would surely break before it could upset such a stone, but a mule-hoof could easily kick it up and over.

Lee faded in among the boulders. He focused his field

glasses on the heights. There was no place a mule could gain those heights. There was a narrow declivity, just about wide enough for a man to struggle up it to the rim. It was like a three-sided chimney slanted at about fifteen degrees. It did not seem to quite reach the rim, but that might be an optical illusion.

Lower down the river gorge, the water washed against broken and tumbled detritus that had scaled from the heights. There was one place where a great sheet of rock had scaled off and fallen into the river athwart the current to form an abutment, behind which the silty water curled and eddied in a mass of yellowish foam. There some hardy water plant or tree had seemingly taken root to thrust up four ungainly looking stalks from what looked like a rounded gravel-bank circled by the yellow foam.

Lee focused the glasses on the plant. "Goddamn," he breathed. The four stalks were the upthrust legs of a dead horse or mule, extended from the gas-bloated belly like stick legs a child might have thrust into the belly of a toy clay animal. Beyond the dead beast there floated in the eddy a pale yellowish rectangle of some sort. The lenses picked out the bold black lettering on it—COPA DE ORO MINE.

Lee squatted in the hot shade, studying the river. He pictured twelve frightened mules driven into the rushing current to swim across at a transverse angle, heads held high, nostrils flaring redly, eyes wide with fright. Some of them must have made it across, but others had not. He looked upriver to where he had seen the overturned stone and estimated how much force the river had had against the laden mules to slant them across the river. Theoretically, if a mule swam strongly across the river, he would have reached the other side just about where the declivity reached the water's edge. Those that had not made it would have been swept downriver to be sucked under by quicksands or drowned. One of them had not gotten very far.

Beyond the heights was a never-never land that no Paiute in his right mind, and few white men, for that matter, would enter. To the Paiutes, it was a forbidden land—the haunt of evil tribal spirits of ferocious and murderous intent. To a white man, the principal deterrents were the heat, the almost utter lack of water, and the trackless barrens themselves. Men had been known to go in there and not to return. Some of them still lay in there, unburied and dried to mummies in faded clothing, staring up at the brilliant sun with eyeholes that could not see. Some of them had bullet holes in the backs of their skulls. Lee knew. . . . It was not a good place.

The hawk drifted high over the gut of the gorge, resting his wings on the updraft of air from the gorge. He floated over the heights on the other side of the river. Suddenly he tilted his wings and swept away from the heights to cross the river to the Arizona side. His slight shadow passed over the hidden man on the Arizona side but the hawk did not see him. Something up on the heights had frightened the hawk. There was only one thing that could put fright into a hawk in that country—*man*.

"Queho," said Lee softly.

Time ticked past in that place where time meant nothing. Nothing moved except the river and the heat-shimmering atmosphere, and the heat in the gorge grew and grew. Queho was up there watching the Arizona side of the river as Lee was watching the Nevada heights.

The long afternoon crept by. Lee sometimes dozed with his half-cocked Winchester across his thighs and his drawn Colt lying beside his right hand.

The long shadows came to ink in the river gorge and after a while they blotted it out altogether. Overhead, the sky was a long, narrow tapestry of mingled blue-gray stippled with twinkling diamond-chips of stars. The river rushed on, effectively drowning out the soft footfalls of Lee as he went to get his roan horse.

The box canyon brooded in a graveyard quiet. Lee stopped short. He faded into cover and made his catlike way up a slope to fatten the deep shadow of an upright boulder.

There was no sound from the picketed roan. Suddenly, he turned his head and looked toward the river, softly cursing the sound of it that overlay all other sounds.

Lee tested the brooding night with eyes, ears, and nose. A faint, rank odor drifted to him—*man*.

Lee catfooted into the darkness with his Winchester at hip-level, muzzle probing the way. The man-odor seemed to have passed from the box canyon.

He stumbled over the sprawled body of the roan. A questing hand went into the raw, hot, wet wound that had completely severed the throat. He was gone from that place of sudden death in seconds.

Minutes ticked past. There was no sound or movement other than the river.

Lee went back to the roan. The saddlebags had been taken. The two big blanket-covered canteens were missing. In a few seconds, Lee Kershaw was also missing.

He moved like wind-driven smoke through the darkness toward the river, his rifle at low port, fully cocked and ready for a snap-shot. He would only get one chance, for Queho would fire at the muzzle flash and he would not miss.

Lee went to ground, trying to skylight any movement against the blue-gray of the night sky. He saw nothing.

The night wind was now questing down the dark river gorge. It moaned a soft threnody over the more sullen murmuring of the Colorado.

Lee paused under a rock ledge whose upper edge overhung his head. He looked down toward the river. As his eyes became more accustomed to the darkness about him, he noticed something different on the light-colored ground in front of him. It had not been there when he had stopped under the ledge. It was a long shadow—the shadow of a tall man who was standing on the ledge *directly over Lee's head*.

The wind shifted. A faint odor came to Lee's questing nose—a mingled aura of sour grease, stale sweat, and an indefinable musky animal-like odor—*Queho*.

Lee slowly raised his rifle. The metal-shod butt clicked sharply against the rock behind him. Gravel pattered down about him as he leaped forward and swung for the killing shot. He saw only the faintest of silently moving shadow. The Winchester exploded stabbing flame and smoke toward the shadow. The smoke blew back into Lee's face. The shot echo slam-banged between the gorge walls and went racketing down the river.

Something splashed. Lee ran toward the river. It was like looking into a trough of India ink. He stood there with the water swirling about his calves, feeling his feet sinking a little too swiftly into the bottom. He sucked back a foot and threw himself toward the shore, just as he realized he had stepped into the edge of quicksand. He crawled up the slope and went to ground behind a ledge.

Minutes ticked past.

A coyote howl came from the heights across the river. Lee just about picked it up over the sounds of the river and the night wind, but he heard it and knew it for the voice of a man, no matter how well it was mimicked.

Lee let down the hammer of his rifle to half-cock. He went back to the broken rock formations and found a hideout in which to sleep until daylight. Queho would not be back across the river that night.

When the faintest gray pearl of dawn light crept into the gorge, Lee focused his field glasses on the opposite side of the river about where the declivity rose to the heights. As the light grew, he saw the shape of the little canvas-covered flatboat moored between rocks at the base of the declivity and partially hidden by brush, probably transplanted there by Queho, for there was no other brush anywhere along the base of the heights.

Lee slid his Winchester forward. He could just make out the thick rope that moored the boat to a stake driven into the gravel. His first shot split the stake. His second cut the rope. The boat floated out into the river, and before it swirled fifty yards ten more rounds of .44/40 slapped through the thin canvas-covered sideboards of the boat from side to side. As the last echoes of the fusillade died out and the gunsmoke drifted away, the boat filled with water and sank from view in a swirling eddy.

Lee crawled back into the rock formation. He cut a chew of Wedding Cake and stuffed it into his mouth. By the time he had the "sauce" worked up, he was paralleling the river behind the rock ledges as he headed downstream to keep close to the only supply of water for thirty miles.

NINETEEN

AMY QUICKLY RAISED her head from her pallet. "Listen!" she cried out in the darkness, but the faint and distant rifle shot echo had died away before the other women awoke.

"What was it?" asked Mildred.

"A shot!"

"Maybe you're hearing things."

"No! I heard it! I wasn't asleep!"

Amy got up and walked out of the cave to step up behind the rampart. The *malpais* land was dark and quiet. Only the night wind moved.

"It could have been Queho," suggested Lucille.

Amy shook her head. "He wouldn't give himself away this close to his hideout."

"Maybe he's hunting," Lucille brightly added.

"At night?" asked Amy.

"Maybe someone is hunting *him*," put in Mildred.

Amy nodded. "They can't get near him during daylight." She looked back at the two pale faces in the dimness. "Maybe we can go down there and find the men who are hunting him."

"You know what happened the last time we tried that," reminded Mildred.

"I won't go this time," said Lucille. "And you can't make me go either!"

Amy stepped down and looked at her. Mildred caught Amy's eye and shrugged as the girl went back into the darkness of the cave. Lately she had seemed strangely content, adapting herself very well to the confined life of the cave.

"Well," said Amy, "it's no use trying to get down there in the dark. Maybe we can wait until dawn."

"Unless Queho comes back before then," said Mildred.

"He'll be back," the girl said softly from the darkness. "They can't kill him."

The arched mouth of the cave was faintly limned in grayness when Queho came silently over the rampart and into the cave. A pair of saddlebags hung over his shoulder. He squatted at the bend of the cave and lighted a candle. He unbuckled the saddlebag straps and dumped out the contents of the bags. Bottles clinked on the hard floor. Queho picked up a bottle and pulled out the cork with his strong white teeth. He drank deeply.

"He's killed someone again," breathed Amy.

"I said they couldn't kill *him,*" the girl whispered in fearful excitement.

In a little while he hurled the empty bottle into the rear of the cave. He lighted a cigar he took from the loot. The alternate flaring up and dying away of the tip of the cigar first glowed against his dark face, then cast it into shadow again.

The light grew from the mouth of the cave. A rataplan of gunfire echoed and re-echoed in the gorge. Queho jumped to his feet and snatched up his Winchester. He ran toward the mouth of the cave, stamping hard on Lucille's outflung right hand. She whimpered in pain. He jumped down behind the rampart, then up onto the step, thrusting the rifle forward and working the action.

The women lay silently. Lucille mouthed her trampled hand, fighting back the tears and sobs.

"He'll want a woman soon," prophesied Mildred.

"With all that liquor in him he won't be able to do any woman any good," said Amy, the professional.

"If he does want a woman," said Mildred, "you go, Amy. After all, it *is* your line of business, isn't it?"

"He doesn't pay," countered Amy.

"He's feeding you," argued Mildred.

"He's keeping all three of us alive," put in the girl.

Queho let the hammer of the rifle down to half-cock. He staggered a little as he came into the cave. He leaned the rifle against the wall and swept the guttering candle aside with one hand, plunging the rear of the cave into semidarkness. He slowly stripped off his filthy clothing. He stood there, naked and hairy, swaying back and forth on his bare feet. He opened the second bottle of booze and drank a third of it, his throat working convulsively.

"It won't be long now," whispered Mildred to the girl.

"He'll never make it," said Amy.

"A lot you know," jeered Mildred.

He turned and walked toward them. He ripped back the blanket that covered the girl and clawed away her thin nightdress. He stared down at her small, red-budded breasts. She lay there, staring almost hypnotized into his strange, dark face. He picked her up and carried her to his odorous pile of blankets and skins.

Amy sat up. "Take me," she offered. The bare heel caught her alongside the jaw and flung her back against the wall.

Queho pawed weakly at the girl. Then he slowly got to his feet and stood there swaying. Then he fell heavily across her thin body and lay still.

Amy wiped the blood from her mouth. "I told you," she said.

The girl lay motionless beneath Queho. The smelly, sweating hulk of the breed and the warm, wet flesh was close against her white nakedness.

Mildred picked up an ax. She walked deliberately toward the bed. Amy stepped in front of her. "This is our chance!" snapped Mildred. "You crazy bitch!" retorted Amy. "If you kill him we may never find our way out of here! There's only enough water left for today! He always makes damned sure of that!"

Mildred slowly lowered the ax. "Christ, but he stinks! Like an uncleaned cage in a zoo!"

"Get up, kid," said Amy to the girl. "It's all over."

Lucille did not move. There was almost a dreamlike look on her narrow face. The weight of the stinking male animal on her felt good. She had never been naked with a male before; she hadn't lied about that.

"Get up, damn you!" cried Mildred.

Amy rolled the breed over against the cave wall. "No use waiting, honey," she said quietly to the girl. "He can't do any woman any good today."

"I wonder if he ever could?" questioned Mildred.

Amy looked quickly at her. "What do you mean?"

Mildred dropped the ax. "Nothing," she hastily replied.

Lucille got slowly to her feet and passed her thin hands down her small, spare body. She walked to her pallet and began to dress.

"Aren't you going to wash the stink from you?" asked Mildred.

Amy watched the girl. "We haven't got enough water," she said. Lucille turned away from them and finished dressing.

Queho mumbled in his stupor.

"What's he saying?" asked Mildred.

Amy held her nose and bent close to Queho. He mumbled again and again. She stepped back. "One word," she said, "over and over—Kershaw, Kershaw, Kershaw." She looked at Mildred. "The only Kershaw I know of is Lee Kershaw, the manhunter."

"My God!" cried Mildred.

"What does it mean?" asked Lucille.

"Lee Kershaw was the man who was with that stinking breed at Fort Mohave when the two of them tried to rape me, anyway Queho did. Kershaw was too drunk to know much about anything, but he wasn't so drunk that he could not kill the engineer of the *Mohave* who had bravely come to my rescue. Well, they put Kershaw and Queho away for twenty years in Yuma Pen. *That* took care of *them!"*

Amy shook her head. "Only Lee Kershaw," she corrected Mildred.

"They were friends?" asked Lucille.

Mildred shrugged. "I suppose so. Kershaw treated that breed as though he was human."

Amy nodded. "That sounds like Lee Kershaw all right."

Mildred looked quickly at Amy. "How well did you know him?"

Amy shrugged. "I worked in Tucson some years back. I knew him fairly well."

"A customer of yours, no doubt?" sneered Mildred.

Amy nodded. "I liked him," she said simply. She looked at Mildred. "You just said the two of them tried to rape you, at least Queho. I thought Queho had been sentenced *for* raping you."

Mildred looked quickly away. "I'll make the breakfast," she volunteered. It wasn't like her to volunteer for any work around the cave.

Amy looked through the items from the saddlebags. She held up a polished-steel mirror. Etched crudely on the back of it was one word—KERSHAW. "This is a prisoner's mirror," she said. "I've seen them before. These must be Kershaw's saddlebags."

"And Queho has killed him," said Mildred. "Maybe he escaped too."

"If he had, why would Queho kill him?"

Mildred wiped the sweat from her face. "How the hell should I know! I'm glad if he did, that's all!"

Amy shook her head. "He hasn't killed him," she said.

"How do you know?" asked Lucille.

Amy shrugged. "If he did kill Kershaw, who did that shooting after daylight down in the gorge?"

"Someone looking for us," said Mildred. "I wish to God Queho and Kershaw had killed each other."

Amy stood up with the mirror in her hand. "He did not kill Lee Kershaw," she said. "I think Kershaw is somewhere along the river looking for us."

Mildred laughed. "The heat is getting to you, sister!" For a moment she eyed Amy, then looked quickly away. "Kershaw is either in Yuma Pen, or he's dead."

Amy slowly polished the mirror against her dress as she walked to the mouth of the cave. She picked up Queho's powerful field glasses and uncased them as she stepped out into the bright morning sunlight beyond the mouth of the cave. She looked over the rampart and focused the glasses down toward the river gorge. "My God!" she cried back over her shoulder. "I can see a man walking on the other side of the river!"

"Let me see," said Mildred. She snatched the glasses away from Amy and refocused them. A lean, bearded man was walking easily downriver on the Arizona side. She could not see his face but the easy, catlike walk seemed familiar.

Amy turned the steel mirror toward the sun and began to flash it.

"What the hell are you doing?" demanded Mildred.

The flashes were shards of the purest silver and could be seen for miles.

Mildred walked back into the cave. A moment later she came out again. "Get down," she ordered.

"He'll be out of sight in a minute!"

Something double-clicked behind Amy. She looked down into the twin black muzzles of a shotgun and along the fat-polished barrels into a pair of glacial blue eyes. "Get down, damn you," repeated Mildred, "or I'll blow off your head!"

Amy lowered the mirror and stepped down. She walked into the cave. She looked back at Mildred. "Why?" she asked.

"It's really none of your business."

"It is when my life and future depend on it. That man

down there was Lee Kershaw. He might be the only hope we have of getting out of here alive."

"I'd get no more mercy from Kershaw than I would from that drunken animal lying there."

"Why? Because you railroaded the two of them into Yuma Pen?"

"I don't have to answer any of your damned questions!" Mildred walked toward the rear of the cave and out of sight.

"Why did you ask her that?" asked Lucille.

"Because she seems more afraid of Kershaw than she does of Queho."

"But why? I don't understand."

Amy shrugged. "I'd like to know the truth about what happened back there on the *Mohave* the night Kershaw and Queho were supposed to have gone on a drunken debauch and tried to rape *Mrs.* Felding. I'm wondering now if Queho raped her, or even *tried* to rape her."

"I don't think so," said Lucille quietly.

Amy studied her. "Why do you think he didn't?"

"Well, he hasn't touched any of us yet, has he?"

"You might have something there. However, he hasn't been around too much."

"Of course," coyly added Lucille. "he *did* try with *me*. I wonder why? With two experienced women of the world like you and Mildred, why would he want *me?*"

Amy looked curiously at the girl. "How would I know? There's something he wants from us. God knows what it is. It must be more than just a bed partner."

"I think I know," replied the girl. "He wants one of us to want him for *himself.*"

Amy wiped the sweat from her face. "It's too deep for me, kid."

"He's too deep for anyone to understand, and yet that is what he wants. Perhaps that is what Kershaw tried to give him—understanding."

Amy nodded. "Lee Kershaw would be the one to do it,"

she agreed. "God knows Lee Kershaw is so deep himself he might just be the one person who ever understood Queho."

"Oh, I don't know!" cried Lucille.

Amy patted the girl's thin, plain face. "God help you," she murmured. She picked up the field glasses and walked outside into the brilliant, metallic-looking sunlight. She focused the glasses on the Arizona side of the river. The river had been turned into a flow of mercury by the bright sunlight. Nothing moved on the far side of the river. Amy walked back into the cave.

Lee Kershaw lay belly-flat behind a piece of forked driftwood driven into the gravelly shore. He had seen the brilliant flashing of reflected sunlight from the forbidding heights across the river. He placed a long branch into the fork of the stick, pointed approximately to where he had seen the flashing. He lay flat behind a ledge and hat-shaded his field glasses to keep them from reflecting the sunlight as he studied the heat-shimmering land across the river. He studied the terrain foot by foot but could not see any sign of man over there.

The sun was beginning to cook his back. Nothing moved across the river, but the heat-disturbed air wavering upward from the baking rock. Lee vanished into the broken rock terrain back from the shore. The river rushed on. The heat waves shimmered. Nothing else moved.

TWENTY

THE UPPERWORKS OF the steamer *Mohave* gleamed like a sepulcher in the soft light of the dusk. The river whispered along its sides. Long bars of gold were thrown on the dark surface of the river from the lighted windows of the steamer. A thread of smoke rose from the galley stack and drifted downstream. The *Mohave* was moored alongside a sandbank that was itself separated from the Arizona side of the river by a narrow and shallow channel.

"Ahoy, the steamer!" hailed Lee Kershaw from behind a boulder. He kept his head down. All steamers passing up or down the river, to Callville at the mouth of the Virgin River, the head of navigation, now kept armed guards on the alert when they were tied up for the night—because of Queho.

"Who is it?" called out a guard.

"Is Captain Mellen aboard?"

"Of course he is!"

"Tell him it's Lee Kershaw!"

"Show yourself, Kershaw!" called out Mellen from the deck in front of the pilothouse.

Lee thumb-snapped a match into flame and lighted his bearded face. He quickly blew out the match.

"Come on aboard!" invited Mellen.

Lee splashed through the shallow water to the sandbank. He gripped the railing of the steamer and easily swung himself up onto the freight deck. He walked up the ladders to the pilothouse. Mellen thrust out a strong hand. "I heard you had come up this way, Lee."

"When do you go upriver?"

"We're waiting for a rise. We passed the *Cocopah* yesterday on her way downriver. She had to turn back from about here because of low water." Mellen waved Lee to a chair on the deck in front of the pilothouse. He handed him a cigar and lighted it for him. "What the hell are you doing around here on foot?"

"Queho outsmarted me. Killed my horse and got away with my food and canteens. Took me almost two days to walk out of that damned furnace."

"You get a crack at him?"

"Only a snap-shot. He was like a shadow, Jack."

"You giving up the hunt?"

"To go back to Yuma Pen?" Lee looked up the shadowy river. "I either get Queho, or I go back to Yuma."

"Or he gets you." Mellen reached inside the pilothouse and brought out a bottle and two glasses. "Look, Lee," he quietly added. "Wait until we get our rise. I'll take you up river to Callville. You can get to Salt Lake City from there before anyone in Arizona Territory gets wise. Who's to know? I'll keep my mouth shut. You know damned well I never bought that story about you trying to rape Milly Felding and killing Jim Anderson."

"You found my Colt in my hand with one cartridge expended and your engineer dead in the water with a bullethole in his head," said Lee quietly. "Besides, I gave my word. When is the rise due?"

"We could see the storm over the mountains toward the northeast late this afternoon. I figure the rise should be here about two hours before the dawn."

"When will you reach the Gut?"

"About an hour after dawn."

Lee drained his glass. The whisky hit his guts like the blow of a mailed fist. "I want you to leave early, Jack. Can you drop me off on the Nevada side of the Gut?"

"Yes, but you'll need a horse, won't you?"

"No. I'll never get within shooting distance of Queho by riding a horse."

Mellen refilled the glasses. "You're a strange one, Lee. I don't think you harbor any hatred for Queho."

"When the time comes, Jack, I'll execute him as neatly as though he was dropped through the gallow's trap at Yuma Pen."

Mellen shrugged. He looked upriver. "Dangerous enough in full daylight and almost impossible in darkness."

"You can do it if anyone can."

"He'll hear us coming upriver."

"He knows this is the time of the year for the high water this far up the river. He'll be expecting to hear steamers now. If you don't stop, he'll never know the difference."

"You have a place to land? I can't put you ashore in there in a small boat, at least on the Nevada side of the river."

"I have a place," replied Lee.

Mellen nodded. "We'll try then."

Lee drained his glass and stood up. "I'll need some canvas and rope for slings, and food, tobacco, whiskey, and a canteen."

"Can do," Mellen said. "What's the canvas for?"

"A shroud for Queho."

"I knew I shouldn't have asked."

Later, as Lee was half-asleep in the same cabin where Milly Felding had made her late evening appearance to send Queho and Lee to Yuma Pen for twenty years, he thought he heard a rise in the pitch of the sucking and gurgling of the river along the side of the steamer.

The hand shook Lee awake. "Time," warned Mellen. "We're getting up steam."

"How's the river?"

"Rising steadily."

Lee slung his Winchester over a shoulder. He slung a canvas pack over the other shoulder and fastened a coil of rope to his belt in the middle of his back. He walked out onto the darkened deck and looked over the side. The sandbar he had crossed the night before was now under two feet of swiftly rushing water. He walked up the ladder to stand on the larboard side of the pilothouse.

The *Mohave* tugged at her moorings in the suck of the rising river. Mellen handed Lee a cigar and cupped a lighted match about the tip of it. "You'll have just about enough time to smoke that," he said. He lighted a cigar for himself and leaned from a side window. "Cast off aft there!" he ordered. He placed a negligent hand on the huge steering wheel that had the lower half of it sunken into the pilothouse deck. A fire door clanged from the main deck. The sound of hissing steam came from the exhaust valves. "Cast off forrrard!" commanded Mellen.

The inshore current got in between the starboard bow of the steamer and the nearby shore, and the *Mohave* began to swing slowly outward toward the center of the river. Mellen spoke into the voice tube. "Slow, ahead, Mac," he ordered.

The *Mohave* trembled like a hound dog evacuating peach stones as power was applied to the great Pitman beams that crank-turned the big stern wheel. The hissing of the slow-speed, cross-compound engine became louder and yet louder. The bows swung out toward midstream to meet the full rushing current of the rapidly rising Colorado.

Mellen judged the speed and power of the current. The river was almost holding the steamer in neutral. He whistled into the voice tube. "Half-speed ahead, Mac," he ordered. The stern wheel began to churn faster and faster, thrashing the dark water into creamy, frothing yellowish-white foam. The mutted *sssoooo-hhhaaaa, sssoooo-hhhaaaa, sssoooo-hhhaaaa* of the engine echoed louder from the higher land on the Nevada side of the river. The dark mouth of the first gorge loomed ahead of the slowly moving *Mohave*.

Mellen eyed the looming sides of the gorge. As the *Mohave* poked her blunt nose cautiously into the darkness, Mellen tugged hard on the whistle cord. The wet-sounding squawking of the whistle bounced an echo back and forth between the gorge walls. Mellen listened attentively.

"What the hell was that for?" snapped Lee. "You want the whole goddamned world to know we're coming?"

Mellen was not listening to Lee. He tugged twice at the whistle cord and listened again to the echoes. He shifted the big wheel and grinned sideways at Lee. "Nervous?" he asked. "Look." He pointed to starboard. A great rock-outcropping rose ten feet from the roiled surface of the river, rimmed with foam, like the foamy fang of a mad dog. "We'd have ripped out our bottom on that if I hadn't picked up the right-sounding echo from the other side of the river."

"Sorry," apologized Lee. Maybe he *was* nervous.

The *Mohave* slogged upriver at a steady pace with the whistle blasting hoarsely now and again. The fire doors clanged, and the chunk wood was hurled into the fires. The paddle wheels thrashed, and the racketing sound of the engine, working at full speed now, came echoing back from the gorge walls.

"How much further along, Lee?" asked Mellen. He pointed to the sky. The first flush of the dawn light was showing.

The *Mohave* entered the gorge. To larboard, or port, the rock walls rose sheer for nearly two hundred feet and to starboard the ground was broken away, eroded and tumbled into the river to form a loosely compacted steep-to bank. An uneasy feeling came over Lee. He had not figured in a rise in the river when he had planted his driftwood markers pointing to the approximate position of the place where he had seen the sun-reflected flashings.

"I hope, for my professional reputation," said Mellen, "that I'm not making this look too easy."

Lee shook his head. "That damned gorge ahead looks as though Charon himself would not attempt to ferry anyone across it."

"Charon?" asked Mellen. "The name is not familiar. What rives does he pilot on?"

"The Styx," drily replied Lee.

"Where's that?"

"Between here and hell."

Mellen nodded. "I know what you mean."

The dawn light was beginning to fill the gorge.

"Where's your landing?" asked Mellen.

Lee climbed over the railing and stood at the very edge of the hurricane deck, looking up the gorge with the faint wraith of smoke hanging about his face from the stub of cigar in his mouth. There should be a ledge of lighter-colored rock on the Nevada side that led to a V-shaped access to the rim of the heights.

"When?" asked Mellen.

Lee took the risk. He could not see his driftwood marker. Where he had placed the marker was now under five feet of swiftly rushing water. "There," he said, pointing ahead to the ledge.

"How will you get back out?" asked Mellen. He whistled into the speaking tube. "Stand by for Slow Ahead, Mac," he warned.

"When are you due downriver?"

"In two days."

"Can you time your passing through the Gut to about dusk?"

"I'll risk it for you, Lee."

"Look for me then, Jack. I may not be alone."

"Who'll be with you?"

"Three women—I hope."

"Slow Ahead!" shouted Jack into the voice tube, and at the same time he swung the wheel to steer the steamer close under the sheer wall. "Now!" he yelled at Lee. *"Vaya con Dios,* Lee!"

Lee leaped. He landed crouched and catfooted on the ledge. The edge crumbled. He caught hold with one hand as his feet went out from under him. His rifle sling slipped from his shoulder and the Winchester plunged into the river. He caught hold with his other hand as his holding hand slipped and the pack sling slipped from his shoulder. The pack followed the rifle into the depths. Lee hooked a moccasined heel over the ledge and swung his body upward. His Colt slipped from its holster and fell into the river.

The *Mohave* whistled as she passed beyond sight around the bend in the river. Lee worked his way onto the ledge and lay bellyflat. There was just enough room for his body. Rock crumbled from the edge as he moved a little. Inch by inch he reached back and loosened the coil of rope from his belt. He looped the rope about a projection and then about his body. He spat out the cigar stub and felt for the makings. He shaped a quirly and then lighted it. He looked sideways across the river toward the Arizona side. It did not look familiar. He looked behind his shoulder to see that the ledge petered out against the sheer rock-wall. He looked ahead. The ledge vanished twenty feet in front of him.

He closed his eyes and rested his head on his forearms. He had landed on the wrong ledge.

...tain know or mean, and then it was going
racted scarcely ten feet, yet, and it put it was
mine cached between the ravines and saw them

TWENTY-ONE

THE HOARSE SOUND of the steamer's whistling came faintly through the gorge. Queho raised his head from his bed. He stood up, naked except for a breechclout, and reached for a rifle. He snatched up his field glasses as he ran to the mouth of the cave. He focused the glasses on the gorge, but by this time the steamer had passed out of sight upriver.

"What was it?" whispered Mildred.

"Steamer," replied Amy.

"I didn't know they came up this far."

"Only when there is a rise in the river during the summer. That's why we haven't heard one since we've been here. The river must have risen."

"If that's so," said Mildred, "he must be used to it. Why is he out there now?"

"I wish I knew! Quiet! He's coming back!"

He came softly into the cave and quickly dressed. He took his rifle and a full canteen and vanished into the rear of the cave. Amy was out of bed in an instant. She snatched up a candle and some matches and catfooted toward the rear of the cave. She felt her way through the dimness. Now and again she would stop to listen but she heard nothing. The stench of the garbage and the latrine hole sickened her the deeper she got into the passageway.

She waited in the darkness, listening for any sound that would warn her of Queho's presence. Softly she walked into another passageway and tiptoed toward the deep pit at the end of it. She thrust her head over the edge. Far below her she saw a faint glow of light, and then it was gone. Something rattled against the side of the pit, and then it was quiet again. She risked lighting the candle. She felt along the edge of the pit and found a rope ladder runged with iron rods.

Amy ran back to the outer part of the cave and began to dress. "I think I know how he gets out of the cave back there," she said excitedly. "There's a pit with a ladder in it."

"So?" asked Mildred.

"I'm going to find out."

"You'll kill yourself if he doesn't do it."

Amy took a pistol from the ammunition box. She shook a lantern to see if the oil reservoir was full. She slung a full canteen over one shoulder.

"If he sees you he'll kill you," warned Lucille.

"So? It'll be better than sitting around here waiting until he does the job here or we die of thirst."

"He'll be back. He *always* comes back. They can't kill *him!*"

"Listen to her," jeered Mildred. "I'll swear she's got a schoolgirl crush on that stinking animal."

"He's not an animal! He's a human being like the rest of us!"

"Speak for yourself, honey," jeered Mildred.

"Who's coming with me?" asked Amy.

Neither one of them spoke.

Amy nodded. "All right. I'll go alone. If I make it, I'll bring someone back for you two."

"If you do," said Mildred gloomily, "he'll likely kill us and fight it out to the last. They'll never take him alive."

"They won't take him at all!" cried Lucille.

Amy picked up a coil of rope. She walked back into the cave and knelt beside the pit. She tied the rope to the lantern bail and then lighted the lantern and lowered it far down into the pit. "See? There's another passageway down there!"

"With him waiting in it," said Mildred.

Amy pulled up the lantern. "When I reach the bottom, lower the lantern to me." She thrust her long, shapely legs down into the pit to place them on the ladder. *"Adios!"* she said. She descended into the pit.

They sat there listening to her making her way down the ladder. "Send it down," she called up. Lucille reached for the lantern. A hand gripped her wrist. Mildred shook her head. Mildred leaned over the edge of the pit and felt for the ladder. She gripped it and began to haul it up as swiftly as she could.

There was no sound from Amy. She knew the game. She felt inside her dress for candle and matches. She lighted the candle and walked into the narrow passageway.

TWENTY-TWO

QUEHO MOVED NOISELESSLY through the *malpais*.
The sun was slanting down on the river gorge. He passed
through a natural passageway and turned hard right, then
hard left. The sunlight streamed into the opening at the end
of the passageway. He stopped there. The river rushed
through the gorge twenty feet below where he stood. A
rusted bucket and a length of rope lay in a niche above a
large wooden keg he used for settling the silty river water.

Queho focused his field glass up the gorge. He turned and
looked down the gorge. He squatted in the passageway and
shaped a cigarette. He lighted it, all the time watching the
river. There was someone out there. He could *feel* someone
out there.

Fifteen feet above where Queho squatted and smoked,
Lee Kershaw sat on his narrow ledge looking down on the
river. He could not make his way to right, left, or up. His
only possible means of escape was the river. Once in the
powerful liquid grip of the river, he'd have to ride the flood
down through the gorge until he found a place to land
downstream. There were treacherous eddies whirling round
and round, cone-shaped, perhaps a foot or two below the
water level, and he knew damned well if he was sucked
down into one of them he'd never come up again.

"No food, no water, and no way home," said Lee.

He looked upriver. The *Mohave* would not be coming
down for two days.

The sun began to heat up the rock face behind Lee. A

117

man could not last half a day on that ledge in the full sunlight.

"Charon?" Jack Mellen had asked. "The name is not familiar. What river does he pilot on?"

"The Styx," Lee had replied.

"Where's that?" Mellen had asked.

"Between here and hell," Lee had said.

The temperature was already 100 degrees and rising steadily. The heat seemed to be really emanating from the rock behind Lee. It was as though the demons of hell far below the rock surface were stoking up the hellfires to roast Lee Kershaw from his perch.

Once his mind reeled; he was brought around by the rope cutting into his body. He opened his eyes to look directly down into the river, and as he did so, he could have sworn he saw a puff of smoke drift from the face of the rock fifteen feet below him. He eased back onto the ledge and fought with all his willpower to regain his senses.

He peered over the edge. A bucket sailed out and plunged down into the river, only to be hauled up again by its rope, brimfull and banging metallically against the rock face.

"At least I know where he gets his water," murmured Lee.

He wiped the sweat from his burning face. He'd have to risk the river.

Amy slogged through the overpowering heat. It was the same story as before—to enter the *malpais* labyrinth was to lose oneself. She sat down in the hot shade of a boulder and closed her eyes. Her canteen was long empty.

It was the smell that aroused her. She opened her eyes. Queho passed just beyond her, moving as silently as a gecko lizard through the *malpais*. Amy did not move, but she did close her eyes. Thirst clawed roughly in her throat.

Amy cautiously crawled over the baking rock. She worked her way toward the direction from which Queho had come. There was a sort of cave mouth there, hidden unless one was within twenty feet of it. She stood up and walked into it with her pistol in her hand.

She stopped short at the very brink of the river. She picked up the bucket and dropped it into the river.

Lee heard the clanking of the bucket. He leaned far over and saw the woman's arms and the back of her head as she drew up the full bucket.

Lee drew back. He loosened his rope from the rock projection and tied a sheepshank into it just below the loop. He replaced the loop about the projection, then severed one of the three short connecting sections of rope between the loops at each end of the hitch. He drew in hard on the rope, and the hitch held. He eased himself over the crumbling edge of the ledge. Slowly he let himself down hand over hand, then pushed his feet against the side of the rock face and bent his knees. He snapped his legs out straight, and swung out over the abyss to swing back in again, letting the rope run through his hands. He swung into the cave mouth and landed lightfooted right at the very brink of the opening where he had seen the arms of the woman and the water bucket.

Amy dropped the dripping bucket from her mouth and yanked the pistol from within the top of her dress. Lee slapped the pistol to one side and grinned at her. "Hello, Amy," he said cheerfully. "You're a long way from Tucson." She stared dumbfounded at him. "They didn't tell me you were one of the three women taken by Queho," he added. He cupped a big hand under her chin and gently tilted her head a little backward to look into her face. "They called you just a woman," he said. "You understand?" She nodded. She suddenly pressed the side of her face hard against his chest. "Oh God, Kershaw!" she murmured.

He raised her head again. "Where are the others?"

"Still up there, Lee," she replied.

"Can you show me the way?" he asked.

"I'm not sure. Oh, Lee! I just can't go back up there!"

Lee took the pistol. He half-cocked it and opened the

loading gate. He twirled the cylinder. The handgun was not loaded.

Lee took the dangling end of the rope and quickly snapped it upward to release the two loops and the unsevered connecting pieces. The rope fell down and he drew it in, minus about a yard from the other end that still hung from the projecting rock. He coiled the rope. "Is this where he gets all his water?" he asked. He looked into the settling keg. It was full of clear water, with a layer of silt at the bottom.

She sat down on the overturned bucket. "I don't know," she replied. "He only keeps so much up in the cave, maybe two or three days' supply."

Lee nodded. "Anyway, he's got a whole damned river here to get his water. How's his food supply?"

"Enough for months," she said.

"From the Copa de Oro Mine?"

She nodded.

"Weapons?" asked Lee.

She held up her two hands. "About ten. Shotguns, rifles, and pistols. Maybe more. He took a pistol, a shotgun, and a rifle from the stagecoach." She looked up at him. "Mrs. Felding was bringing the rifle back from San Francisco for her husband. Queho said it was yours."

Lee looked quickly at her. "A Sharps .40/70?"

She shrugged. "I don't know. She said it had belonged to her husband originally and he had lost it to you in a crooked poker game. The breech was engraved with the name of Ahvote and a date—I can't remember what it was."

"Maybe it was a date in April, 1881," he suggested.

"That was it, Lee." She wiped the sweat from her face. "I remember he was very angry because it had only three cartridge-cases with it. Mrs. Felding didn't know anything about it."

Lee nodded. "She wouldn't."

"Why was he angry?"

"Because he must reload those three cartridges before he

can fire them. Besides they only last so long after so many loadings, unless he can resize the cases."

"There were all kinds of tools and things in the box with the rifles."

"What about ammunition for the other guns."

"Boxes full," she replied.

"Sounds like he's got an arsenal," Lee commented drily.

She nodded. "And he knows how to use them, Lee."

He squatted and rested his back against the wall, looking at the empty Colt. "Great," he murmured.

"What can you do now?" she asked.

He took out the makings and shaped a cigarette. He placed it between her lips and lighted it. He fashioned another cigarette for himself. "Wait until dark," he finally replied.

"And then?"

"Just wait for Queho."

She paled. "You mean . . . ?"

He nodded. "He'll come looking for you once he knows you're gone. He doesn't know I am here. You're the cheese in the trap, Amy. He'll figure you'll need water. This is the only place where you can get it."

She passed a shaking hand across her sweat-streaked face. "He may think I've gone somewhere else."

"Where? You can't live a day in the barrens back from the river. You can't get down to water for ten miles upstream and another ten miles downstream. And even if you could, where would you go from there? He knows that."

She looked out across the sunlit river to its Arizona side. "I can swim, Lee," she said. "I'm good at it."

He pointed down toward the deceptive-looking cone-shaped eddies swirling around and around like a carousel, dimpling the swiftly rushing water. "Just swim into one of those," he suggested. "You'd never reach the surface again, Amy."

She looked at the lean, bearded face of Lee Kershaw. "What do we do now, Lee?"

"We've got plenty of water and tobacco. We're out of the killer sun. There's a bit of a breeze through here, hot as it is. It could be worse." He grinned. "We can kill the time by you telling me everything that happened to you and the others after Queho kidnapped you. I want to know about his cave, his movements—everything!"

Amy grinned back. "In the beginning . . . ," she started.

TWENTY-THREE

"WOMAN?" THE QUESTIONING tone came faintly into the darkened cave. There was no answer.

"Woman?" the soft call came again.

"Here, Queho," Amy called out faintly.

"Come out here," he ordered.

"I can't," she replied. "I sprained my ankle in the rocks."

It was very quiet. The subdued rushing song of the river sounded in the background.

Lee flattened his back against the side of the cave; the woman did the same, so that the breed could not silhouette them against the lighter area at the river-end of the cave. They could hear the breed's heavy breathing.

"You got gun?" asked Queho.

"No," she lied.

"You lie! Women tell me you got gun! Throw it out!"

She peered at Lee in the dimness. He nodded. She threw the gun clattering on the hard ground at the mouth of the cave.

It was very quiet again. They could no longer hear the breathing of Queho. Lee snapped his head around. The unmistakable odor of the breed had suddenly come to him but he could not see Queho.

"You crawl here, woman," said Queho.

He was only fifteen feet from Lee. Lee nodded. Amy sank down to her hands and knees and crawled toward the unseen breed. Lee could faintly make out Queho as he moved closer to the woman. "Let me see ankle," he said. Lee was startled when Queho thumb-snapped a match into light and bent over the woman. Lee closed in, knife in hand. At the last second, Queho must have been warned for he blew out the match and whirled to fire from the hip. The bullet did Lee no harm, but the blast of flame and smoke from the muzzle of the .44/40 Colt temporarily blinded him. Amy stood up and dragged at Queho's gunarm in the darkness, but he threw her off, as a rat is thrown by a terrior. Queho fired again, but Lee had gone down low and the flame seared across the back of his neck. His head caught Queho in his lean belly and drove the breed hard against the wall. The Colt clattered to the ground.

Queho caught Lee about the throat with his powerful hands and got a knee in the privates for his pains. As he doubled up in agony, a left uppercut snapped back his head and a driving right-cross hurled him toward the mouth of the cave. Lee made the mistake of charging in. A rock bounced from the top of his head, and he staggered back, half-stunned. His left foot went over the brink. He threw himself sideways to drop flat, but he went over the edge and caught hold with both hands.

Queho charged, but the Colt exploded almost in his face. He was not hit but was half-blinded by the flame and smoke, as Lee had been. He whirled and ran from the cave as Amy fired twice more.

It was quiet again except for the rushing of the river.

"Lee!" cried Amy. "Oh God! Where are you, Lee?"

"Here," he called back. "Give me a hand before he comes back!"

Amy made a loop in the rope and handed it to Lee. He caught hold as she passed the rope around a projection in the cave. He pulled himself to the floor of the cave, aided by Amy, and lay flat, breathing hard. "Give me the pistol," he said. She placed the Colt in his hand.

"Will he be back?" she asked.

"Not for a while," he replied. He sat up and half-cocked

the Colt. He snapped open the loading gate and turned the cylinder, feeling the ends of the cartridge cases. He felt only five of them. Queho, as Lee and others did, usually let his pistol hammer rest on an empty chamber. There wasn't a live round left in the cylinder.

"What now?" she asked.

He stood up. "We'll block the cave entrance," he replied.

"Then you're not going to try and find the cave?"

"Hardly," he said. "He knows someone is here now!"

"But does he know it is you?" she asked.

He looked at the pale oval of her face in the darkness. "I think so, Amy. You see, you called me by name. . . ."

They walked into the darkness, pausing now and then to listen, but no one came. Queho had Lee spotted now. He might be waiting out there in the darkness—waiting for his chance. The only retreat for Amy and Lee would be the return of the *Mohave*. If the river dropped suddenly, the steamer would be held upriver until the next rise came, which might not be for days.

"What if the river drops?" asked Amy suddenly.

Lee was startled. It was almost as though she had read his mind. "It won't drop," he replied. "Jack will come by about dusk tomorrow."

"And if he doesn't?"

Lee shrugged as he placed a rock on the barricade. "We'll try inland," he said.

"Not during the daylight. You know he'll be watching."

"Then we go by night."

"What happens the next day? I mean—is there any water inland? How far is it to water?"

Lee fashioned two cigarettes. He placed one in her mouth and lighted it, looking into her anxious eyes. "Jack will show up," he promised.

"You know we can't make it to water inland," accused Amy. "Not in this heat, anyway."

Lee sat down with his back against the wall. "You happen to have any food on you?" he asked.

She shook her head. "I forgot," she replied. "Do you?"

He smiled in the darkness. "In the river," he replied, "along with my rifle, pistol, and about everything else I needed to live in this country."

"Then there's really no hope, is there?"

"There's always hope," he quietly assured her.

After a while, they both slept.

TWENTY-FOUR

"IT'S ALMOST LIKE a ritual," whispered Mildred to
Lucille. Queho squatted in the rear of the cave beside a
lighted lantern. He had the rifle case open in front of him.
The lamplight reflected from the polished breech of the rifle
and from the accouterments and tools. He was selecting
various items from the case.

Queho moved as he heard Mildred's voice. The lamplight
shone on his dark sweating face. He reached up a hand and
wiped his face. It was then the women realized that it was
not sweat on his face, but blood. His shirt, too, was darkly
stained about the left side. His breathing was harsh and
irregular.

"You've been wounded!" cried Lucille. She got to her
feet.

He waved her back. "It's nothing," he said.

"But it *is* something," she insisted. She walked to him
and tilted back his head. His nose had been smashed, and
blood ran freely from it. She placed a hand against his side,
and he winced in pain. "Take off the shirt," she ordered.
Silently he obeyed. The bullet had furrowed his left side just
below the ribs and above the hip. She closed her eyes and
turned away.

"Don't faint," sneered Mildred. "That is, if you plan to
be an angel of mercy."

"Bring me clean cloth and some hot water," said Lucille.
Mildred laughed. "Get it yourself," she said.

The young woman poked up the fire and heated water.

While she prepared to treat Queho, he went back to his "ritual," as Mildred had called it. He set primers into each of the three two-and-a-quarter-inch-long cartridge cases. He filled each of the cases with 70 grains of powder and pressed wads in on top of the powder. He took a dozen 370-grain .40/70 bullets and placed them one at a time in a small vise. Patiently he drilled into the tip of each of the bullets.

Lucille came to him and washed his face. She touched his split lips with a cloth dipped in antiseptic. His nose had stopped bleeding but was still misshapen. She bathed his flesh wound and wrapped a clean cloth bandage about his lean waist. She tied it neatly in place. He shrugged back into his bloody shirt without thanking her. She watched him from the shadows.

Queho opened a box of .22 caliber blank cartridges. He carefully pressed a blank base-down into each of the holes he had drilled into the .40/70 bullets. He lowered the breech of the rifle and inserted one of the bullets, seating it firmly home in the rifling just ahead of the chamber. He slid in a long cartridge case and raised the rifle breech to close it. He filled a canteen and slung it over a shoulder. He took a Colt revolver and loaded it. He placed it in a holster and buckled a gunbelt about his lean waist. He took his field glasses and slung them over a shoulder. He turned and blew out the lantern.

"Go easy on the water," his voice came out of the darkness. "It will take some time to get more."

They did not move. Minutes ticked past. Faintly they heard an iron rung clank against the side of the pit.

"She must be dead," said Lucille at last.

"Serves her right," said Mildred.

Lucille looked at her in the darkness. "I liked her, Mildred."

"She was a whore!"

Lucille did not answer. She lay down.

"I'm more interested in who he's after now," said Mildred.

"Maybe she's still alive."

"No. He's killed her. He wouldn't go to all that trouble with that damned rifle if it was only Amy."

"Maybe she's with the person Queho is after."

Mildred laughed. "Like who?"

"Lee Kershaw," replied Lucille.

There was no comment from Mildred.

The first shot broke the quiet just at the first light of dawn. The bullet passed over the top of the barricade and struck an angle in the cave wall. It exploded on impact, scattering wicked little shards of lead throughout the cave. Lee winced as a shard struck the back of his neck. The woman screamed in terror. Lee placed a hand over her mouth and looked into her widened eyes. "No use in screaming," said Lee quietly. She nodded. He withdrew his hand just as the second shot slapped into the outside of the barricade and exploded. "He knows I'm in here," said Lee as he shaped a cigarette. "He's probably made Express bullets out of his .40/70s. He isn't fooling with us, Amy. He means to mangle and kill." The third shot whipped clear through the cave and across the river. It hit and exploded against a boulder.

Lee sat between the woman and the barricade. It was very quiet. "Maybe he's gone," whispered Amy. Lee shook his head. "Maybe shifting to get a better place to shoot."

Minutes ticked past. Lee bellied toward the barricade. The bullet struck the arch of the cave-opening above the barricade and showered Lee with fragments. He rolled sideways and lay close against the side of the cave. The second shot hit the top of the barricade and exploded. Lee heard the distant booming echo of the rifle rolling away down the canyon. The third shot struck the wall of the cave and exploded. Amy cried out as a fragment bruised her left arm.

Then it was quiet again for a long, long time.

"I think I know," said Amy at last.

Lee looked at her. "Know what?" he asked.

"Why he shoots three times and stops."

"Go on," said Lee.

"When he found the rifle at the stagecoach he was very angry with Mildred because there were only three cartridge cases with it."

Lee nodded. "Figures. Well, he's got all day to do his reloading."

"Maybe he'll run out of bullets."

"He can always mold more."

"Maybe he'll run out of powder."

"He can always empty other cartridge cases."

Amy looked sideways at him. "It's pretty hopeless, isn't it? I mean, it's only a matter of time before he kills us, isn't it?"

Her answer was the distant booming discharge of the Sharps rifle, followed almost instantly by the smashing of the bullet somewhere within the cave or against the barricade.

Queho had not fired for hours. The long dusk shadows filled the gorge.

"Maybe he's gone?" suggested Amy.

Lee shook his head.

"Maybe he thinks we're dead. Why doesn't he come down here?"

Lee shrugged. "Why? Dead or alive he's got us cold."

She laughed.

He eyed her. "What's so funny?"

"He may have us," she replied, "but it sure as hell isn't cold." She wiped the sweat from her heat-reddened face.

The *Mohave* whistled twice upriver.

Lee leaned out from the river side of the cave and waved. He looked back at the woman. "Strip off your skirt," he ordered her. "You'll have to jump."

The paddle wheel of the steamer slowed down, then went into reverse to slow her speed. She swung in toward the heights. There was hardly a yard's clearance. "Jump!

Goddammit! Jump!" yelled Jack Mellen from the pilot-house.

Amy jumped cleanly. Jack whistled as he saw her white underdrawers fluttering as she crossed the gap and landed lightly on the deck. Lee jumped right after her. Jack Mellen swung the big wheel and whistled into the voice tube. "Half-speed ahead, Mac," he ordered. "We've picked up our cargo."

Lee looked into through a pilothouse window. "One down and two to go, Jack," he said. *"Gracias!"*

"Por nada," said Jack as he shifted his cigar. "Is Queho dead?"

"Not yet," replied Lee.

"Thanks, captain," said Amy.

Jack nodded. "My pleasure, ma'am," he said. It was a cinch that she was not the governor's niece *or* Mrs. Felding.

Amy read Jack's mind. "I'm the prostitute," she explained.

Jack tipped his hat. "Pleasure, I'm sure," he murmured. "You can have my cabin, ma'am," he invited.

She shook her head. "Lee and I will share his cabin. We're old friends. We've a lot to talk about on the run downriver."

Jack looked sideways at Lee. Lee was watching Amy walking regally aft toward the cabins with her long upper legs attired only in her underdrawers. She turned. "After all, I do owe you something Lee," she added.

He reluctantly shook his head. "You don't owe me anything, Amy."

"Then come for old time's sake," she offered.

Lee grinned. "I'll do just that," he agreed.

Jack Mellen leaned on the whistle cord and the hoarse, squawking echo carried through the river gorge like the crying of a lost soul.

TWENTY-FIVE

"YOU'RE PRESSING YOUR luck, Kershaw," said the Nevada deputy.

Lee leaned against his sorrel looking toward the east. The terrain was a kaleidescope of color under the late afternoon sun. Far to the east was a dark line of color against the sky. He began to build a cigarette as he watched the possemen leading the three horses up the steep trail. Three dead men lay across their saddles, bobbing stiffly with the motion of the tired horses.

"This is the second time in a week we went in there," continued the deputy. "The first time we never saw him, but we heard some shooting near the river. We couldn't even find the way to the river and ran out of water."

Lee lighted up, watching the dead men and their horses being led toward the road. The faces of the living possemen were taut, and their mouths were like tight seams against the brown of their faces.

"This time we got near the river. All we saw of him was the smoke from his rifle, and from three different places at that. Three times he fired at what I thought was an impossible range, and each time he hit a man. Then, for some crazy reason of his own, he stopped firing, and we managed to get our asses out of there. So help me Christ! Kershaw, if he had kept on shooting he might have gotten us all!"

Lee nodded. "Likely," he admitted.

The dark line was moving swiftly across the barrens.

"He might be watching us right now," added the deputy.

"Possible," said Lee.

"No one can get near him. *No* one! He knows every time someone comes anywhere near his hideout."

Lee nodded. "For sure," he agreed.

"Look, Kershaw: You got one woman out of his hands. Don't press your luck. The other two are likely dead by now anyway."

Lee shook his head. "I don't know that," he said quietly. He looked sideways at the deputy. "Besides, the one I got out there was the one that was least important, at least to the people who made a deal with me to get the women out of there."

"I don't get it."

"Neither do I. But I made a deal. I either get the other two back or I go back to Yuma Pen to finish nineteen and a half years."

"You'll never get near him, I tell you! No man can live in that damned *malpais* country!"

"Queho can," reminded Lee.

"Well, he ain't exactly a *man*, is he?"

"He is—to me."

"You're a strange one, Kershaw."

The dark line was coming closer and moving more swiftly.

"I can't order any of my men to go with you."

"I'll make it alone," said Lee.

"You might get one or two of them to volunteer."

"They'll only get in my way."

"There's a hell of a storm brewing over the *malpais*, George!" called out one of the possemen to the deputy. "By Christ! Lookit them clouds!"

The storm was reaching the far side of the *malpais* country. A cool wind reached the posse and dried the sweat on their faces.

"When will you be back here?" asked Lee.

"Day after tomorrow," replied George.

"For sure?"

"For sure."

Lee nodded. "Look for me then, George." He mounted the sorrel and touched him with his moccasined heels. He rode down the steep trail to reach the grim edge of the *malpais*.

"You crazy!" yelled George. "In an hour the flash floods will sweep through those canyons taking everything with them. You can't live in there, Kershaw!"

Lee looked back. "It'll work for me," he called back. "He can't see me coming through that. It'll supply me with all the water I'll need and it'll drop this damned temperature."

"You'll get a hell of a lot more water than you'll ever be able to use!" shouted George.

"Five feet over his head," drily added a posseman.

Lee Kershaw did not look back. He entered the first canyon and was gone from sight just as the first great, fat raindrops plopped on the dry and thirsty land.

Torrential rains and roaring flash floods were usual in that country at that time of the year, but Lee had never experienced anything like the insane storm that smashed with howling sixty-mile-per-hour banshee winds and a hard-driven rain that struck like the lash of a lead-tipped whip.

The sorrel tried to turn and run with the storm, but Lee forced him on. The closer Lee could get to the river without being seen by Queho, the better his chances would be to get Queho.

Lee raised his head as he rose through a narrow canyon. It was the most dangerous route one could take during such a storm, but he could not get close to the river by any other way, and it would do no good to turn back now.

The roaring sound was subdued at first. Lee looked up at either side of the canyon. There wasn't any chance of getting the horse up out of the canyon that way, and Lee wasn't even sure he could make it to safety himself.

The roaring grew louder, filing the canyon with a

menacing sound. It was close, perhaps just around the next bend. Lee swung from the saddle and reached for his Winchester. He looked back over his shoulder and instantly forgot about the Winchester and everything else except getting his ass out of the way of the roaring wall of muddy water ten to twelve feet high that had swept around the bend in the canyon and was taking everything movable along with it in its mad rush down the canyon.

Lee leaped for the side of the canyon. His feet slipped. He dug clawed hands into the harsh earth and began to pull himself upward. Only once did he look back and that in time to see the sorrel being lifted to the yellowish foaming crest of the flood and then dropped behind and under the water to join the mixed cargo therein—brush, rocks, scrub trees, snakes, lizards and any other living creature that had happened to get in the way—but not Brother Kershaw.

Lee hung on with one hand, waist-deep in the icy churning water that tore at him to break loose his precarious hold. "Let go, you sonofabitch!" he yelled. He managed to pull himself higher as an uprooted tree bore down on him, menacing him with its Medusa-like head of thick outthrust roots.

Lee reached safety. He crawled under an overhanging ledge and yanked off his boots to pour the water from them. He watched the raging flood scouring away at the sides of the canyon. He leaned back and felt for the makings in his shirt pocket. He shaped and lighted a cigarette, sitting there like a fatalistic Paiute as the flood raced by hour after hour, accompanied by an eerie, grinding cacophony of sound and the savage drum-tapping of the rain.

It was dark by the time Lee slid and slopped down to the canyon bottom. The rain had stopped. The sky had cleared. Water was held in every cavity in the ground. It would remain there for two days at least until the forthcoming hundred-degree temperatures and broiling sun would literally suck them dry.

He walked on squelching through the darkness. There

would be a moon that night. More by instinct than any other reason, he climbed a ridge and looked toward where he thought the river should be, and in the first faint light of the moon he saw the river gorge about a mile away.

As the moon rose higher, the rays shone on the wet rock, giving it a cold, glittering appearance. It was very quiet. There was no wind.

Lee stopped behind a boulder. "Beats the hell out of me," he said softly. There was nothing he could recognize. He shoved back his wet hat and placed a chew of Wedding Cake in his mouth; as he did so, he saw a pile of loose, tumbled rock lying in a sort of V-shaped trough. He catfooted forward, stepped over the rocks and into the very cave where he and Amy had been besieged by Queho.

Lee left the cave and found a place to hide. As the moonlight grew against the face of the heights back from the river, he studied the area where he remembered seeing the bright flashings days past. Water was still running from the higher land and trickling over the rimrock to plunge far below to the talus slopes. The moon glittered from the falling water. "Lovely," breathed Lee. He shifted his chew and spat and then raised a hand to wipe his mouth but he arrested the action in midair. There was one place, about halfway down the cliff face where the water dropped but did not continue.

"It's a deep cave," Amy had told Lee. "The mouth of it opens out about midway of a sheer cliff, and part of the mouth is overhung by rock so that the cave itself can't be seen from up above. The cave mouth has a sort of level place that extends out beyond the rock overhang where earth had collected. Queho had dug down into the earth to form a sort of trench, and he had piled rocks just beyond the trench to form a barricade, through which he had made loopholes that he kept plugged with rocks. On each side of the cave mouth the cliff bulged out, so that no one might see into it from either side. Below the barricade was a steep slope of rock that had broken from the cliff face and fallen far below. That is the only way the outer mouth of the cave can be reached by anyone. It is very noisy when anyone walks on it."

"Sonofabitch," murmured Lee. He faded into the broken rock beyond the mouth of the water cave.

The moonlight was bright on the slope. A fly could hardly crawl across it without being seen. Little bright ribbons of water ran down the talus slope, braiding and interbraiding before they reached the bottom.

Somewhere to the left, around the bulging cliff, must be the secret entrance to the natural pit that reached upward to the rear part of the hideout cave. Lee squatted in the shelter of a rock ledge and shifted his chew. Either approach to the cave was dangerous. The slope was moonlighted and noisy. The rear entrance, so to speak, would be dark, and Lee would have to light his way, inviting a bullet out of the dark. It would be better to risk the slope after moonset, noisy as it was. A clattering sound caught his attention. Part of the talus slope had slid hissing down to the bottom of the slope, displaced by the running water. Nothing moved up at the cave mouth.

If he is up there, thought Lee, he would have checked on the noise coming from the talus slope. Or maybe, he added, he knew it was just a slide. Maybe it wasn't the right cave at all. Possibly if it was the right cave, they were all gone. Maybe the two women were dead.

"There's only one way to find out, Kershaw," the mind voice seemed to say to Lee. "Go up there."

The odds were high. But at least he had gotten out of Yuma Pen. He could walk across the barrens that night and the next day, well supplied with rain water in the hollows. It was about forty miles to the Utah line.

"You're a man of your word, Kershaw," reminded the voice.

The talus slide moved again, and some of it slid hissing and rattling down to the foot of it, not more than a hundred yards away from Lee. He looked up at the cave. Nothing moved up there. Damn the moonlight anyway!

Lee walked silently to the foot of the slope where it curved around the bulge of the cliff. He worked his way up the slope, temporarily out of sight of anyone up at the cave but a beautiful six-foot target for anyone behind and below him. Every step he made, as careful as he was, was noisy, and now and again he would start a small slide whereby he would make one step up the slope and slide back two.

He reached the bottom of the cliff and worked his way up toward the cave mouth. Nothing moved up there. Nothing moved on the talus slope.

He pressed close to the side of the cliff, softly cursing the cold, muddy water that dribbled down from high overhead and soaked through his clothing.

Fifty yards from the cave, he stopped to get his breath. He looked down the slope. A man had come out of the rock labyrinth. He wore no hat and walked as silently as a hunting cat, carrying a long rifle at the trail. The clear moonlight glittered on the breech and polished barrel of the rifle.

Lee froze in position. Queho was too far for Lee to risk a pistol shot at him. If he looked up. . . .

Detritus slid down the far side of the talus slope. Queho looked quickly back over his shoulder, but he did not look up toward the tall man who stood with his back against the cliff face looking down at him. Lee could feel the loose rock at his feet starting to move ever so slightly. Queho passed directly below Lee. The slide started the instant Queho had passed out of sight.

Lee worked his way up the slope covered by the rattling, clattering sound of the slide. He reached the rampart and swung up and over it to drop lightly behind it. One of the loopholes had not been plugged. Lee peered through it. Queho again stood at the bottom of the slope looking up toward the cave. Lee froze in position until the breed moved on out of sight.

Lee wiped the cold sweat from his face. The interior of the cave was dark. He felt for his matches and stepped into the dark interior, thumb-snapping a match into flame as he did so.

"Who is it?" cried Mildred Felding.

Lee turned toward her. "Lee Kershaw," he said quietly.

Her face set in sudden fear and her great, vacant blue eyes widened.

Lee looked past her. "Where is the governor's niece?"

Mildred would not answer: she *could* not answer this man. There was a greater fear of him in her than there ever had been of the breed Queho.

Lee turned, and the faint, flickering pool of light fell across the younger woman asleep in a bed that was much wider than the others Lee could see. The smell of the cave clung about Lee like an old familiar coat. "The stink in here makes my eyes smart," he said to no one in particular.

"He might come back," volunteered Mildred at last.

"How does he get into the rear of the cave?"

"There's a natural pit there. He has a rope ladder in it."

Lee nodded. "Amy told me that. Is there any other way?"

"She's still alive?"

"She is."

"Where is she?"

Lee shrugged. "Back in business in Prescott, as far as I know."

"The whore! She's safe enough! What about us?"

Lee looked at her. "I'm here now," he said simply.

"What can you do?" she sneered.

"Get you out of here," replied Lee.

"How much are you being paid?"

Lee slanted his eyes at her. "The highest price in the world," he replied.

"I knew it!" she crowed.

"My freedom," he said.

That shut her up.

Lee lighted a lantern. "Wake her up!" he ordered. "Get dressed. You get outside behind that rock barricade and watch that slope for Queho. Keep your head down!"

Lee looked at the arsenal Queho had proudly racked against the cave wall. He took down the Winchester '73 and filled the magazine with twelve .44/40 cartridges. He took a box of fresh .44/40's and put it into his pocket. He took a coil of light rope.

"Who is he?" cried the girl from behind Lee.

"Lee Kershaw, honey," said Mildred. "He'll get us out of here. Now get dressed."

"What has he done to Queho?" she demanded.

Lee turned slowly at the tone of the girl's voice. He looked at the girl's plain face and then questioningly across her dark head into the eyes of Mildred Felding. She nodded and then shrugged. "It's true," she murmured as she started to dress. "God knows it. . . ."

Lee walked into the rear of the cave. He knelt beside the deep, narrow pit and tied the rope to the lantern bail. He lowered the lantern as far as he could, past the dark mouth of the passageway where the ladder ended. He dropped the stones into the darkness below the feeble lightpool of the swinging lantern and only faintly heard them strike far, far below in the stygian darkness.

Lee pulled up the ladder. He took each gun in turn from Queho's arsenal. The rifles and the shotguns he smashed against the side of the cave bending the barrels. He threw them down into the pit. He removed the cylinders from the revolvers and bent the barrels, then dropped guns and cylinders down into the darkness. He heaved the boxes of stores from the Copa de Oro Mine down on top of the ruined guns and topped the heap by dumping a dozen cans of Kepauno Giant Blasting powder, also from the Copa de Oro Mine, into the pit. The sweat ran from his body.

"Why?" asked the girl.

Lee turned to look at her. "Simple strategy," he replied as he lighted a cigar he had found in a box among Queho's stores. "I'm destroying his arsenal and his base of supplies. I wish to God I could dry up the Colorado River so that he'd be out of water too."

She searched his lean, bearded face. "What will happen to him?"

Lee shrugged. "He won't be my problem when I get you women out of here."

She studied his face and looked into his eyes. "That's not true," she corrected him. "He *is* your problem. He's society's problem."

Lee shook his head. *"He's* a problem to society all right, but not the way you put it. Don't you understand? There never was a place for him in our society and he has made it impossible for himself to return there. He has tried to create his own little world here, and he has failed."

"Couldn't you have let him have it?"

Lee shrugged. "When he killed, as he has done, he left no place for himself, even *here*. He'll have to pay the penalty, ma'am."

"Are you his judge and jury?" she fiercely demanded.

Lee shook his head. "Not even his executioner. That is, not if I can help it." He walked past the girl toward the mouth of the cave. "Anything moving out there?" he asked Mildred.

"Nothing but dripping water," she replied.

"We'll wait until it is dark, then risk the slope. We'll have to move fast. He may hear our descent, but he won't be able to see us. We'll have to keep moving all night and hide out by day. He knows this area like the palms of his dirty hands."

She nodded. "The girl and I could stay here while you hunted him down, Kershaw."

Lee shook his head. "My job is to get the both of you out of here. I made no deal to kill Queho."

"But there must be a reward for him. Wouldn't that be worth your while?"

Lee relighted his cigar. "All I want is my freedom. After

I get that, I don't give a goddamn what they do about Queho. Let someone else track him down and kill him."

"You know there is no one but you who can do that."

"It's not for me."

She searched his face. "Are you afraid?" she sneered.

Lee fanned out the match. "Maybe," he admitted. "God knows, I never really expected to get you women out of here."

"We're not out of here yet!"

He nodded. He turned and walked into the cave. The girl was not in sight. He walked to the rear of the cave and past the pit until he found the noisome combination garbage and latrine room. The girl was not there. He looked up several blind passageways to find them empty. It wasn't until he found the ladder again hanging down into the deep pit that he knew where she had gone.

TWENTY-SIX

"GET DOWN THE slope," ordered Lee. *"Now!"*

The woman was badly frightened. "But it's like daylight! She will have told him by now that you're here!"

"All the more reason we've got to get out of here now! I don't plan to have him keep us holed up here until we run out of water, and he can damned well do it with that rifle of his."

"It's my *husband's* rifle!" she protested.

"Git!" he snapped.

Mildred got!

Lee picked up the last can of Kepauno Giant powder and a length of fuse. He sat astride the rampart and looked down the slope as the woman, softly cursing, made her way down the slope. There was no sign of life anywhere beyond the foot of the slope. It might take time for the girl to find Queho, and time for him to get back to the cave area, and in that time Mildred and Lee must be out of sight and under cover.

Mildred slipped and sat down on her broad rump. Like a child on a slide, she moved swiftly down the slope, accompanied by the clattering and hissing of the wet talus as it moved downward.

"Good going, Milly," thought Lee aloud. He grinned. "That broad rump of yours is good for something else after all."

Mildred reached the bottom of the slope and was smart enough to head at once for cover. Lee dropped to the slide and worked his way, part walking and part sliding, over toward the bulge in the cliff, with his eyes always on the lower ground. He reached the foot of the slide and melted into cover near Mildred. She lay face downward on the wet and muddy ground, and her breathing, more from fear than from exertion, was harsh and irregular.

"This way," said Lee.

"Damn you! Let me rest!"

"Move," he said implacably.

Mildred moved.

Lee scouted the entrance to the water cave. Nothing moved. He looked back at the woman. "Do you know how to shoot?" he asked.

She nodded. "Will taught me."

He gave her the Winchester. "It's at half-cock," he said.

"I know."

He jerked his head. "Get in among the rocks."

"There are rattlesnakes in there!"

He shrugged. "Get bit or get shot," he said. "Makes no difference to me."

She chose the danger of rattlesnakes.

Lee walked into the tunnel. He dumped the bucket and rope into the moonlit river. He shoved the settling keg in after the bucket and the rope. He placed the fused can of blasting powder within the entrance amidst the rubble of his improvised barricade and piled the rock atop the powder can. He fed the fuse out to where Mildred waited for him. He looked about. "Go that way," he said, pointing toward the west.

"Is that the way we get out of here? How far do we have to go?"

He nodded as he struck a match. "Through that canyon— maybe fifteen miles."

"Do we go tonight?"

He shook his head. "I've got to find Lucille," he replied.

"Forget about her! What about *me!* Are you willing to take the risk of losing *me* again just to save her?"

He looked at her. "I'll admit it's a hard decision to make," he drily replied, "but I made a deal with your husband *and* the governor. The deal was to get all three of you women out of here."

"You got two out! Isn't that enough?"

He applied the match to the fuse. "You're not out of here yet, lady," he replied. He grinned. "Better start running west, though, or maybe you won't get out of here at all."

She ran. Lee grinned at the familiar rump action of hers.

The explosion blew a cloud of dust and broke rock out of the cave entrance like a blast from a gigantic shotgun barrel. The thunderous echo bounced from the sheer cliffs on either side of Queho's cave and started a massive rushing of talus down the great slope. The echo slam-banged back and forth between the rock walls as it reluctantly died down the long canyon that led to the outer world. Then it was quiet again. The dust drifted in the now windless air and slowly dissipated.

Lee lay bellyflat between two boulders, with his elbows propped on the ground and his hands grasping Queho's powerful field glasses. The moonlight made the wet slopes and heights sharp and clear to the eye. Nothing moved. It was like a lunar landscape or the dream landscape of an artist mystic.

Lee focused the glasses on the cave high above the talus slope. There was no one there. Nothing moved.

"This is crazy," the woman whispered hoarsely from behind Lee. "The girl is lost! Gone! If he hasn't taken her with him he's killed her. Let's get out of here while we can!"

He shook his head. "I have to know," he said.

"You'll get your damned pardon! I'll see to that!"

He looked back at her. "I'll just *bet* you will, Milly." His hard, gray eyes forced her empty blue ones to turn away. "As long as I am the only one, outside of Queho, who knows the truth of what happened aboard the *Mohave*, you'll always be in fear of me, eh?"

"What the hell are you talking about?" she demanded.

"The truth, Milly, just the truth."

"You'll get your pardon!"

He nodded. "You're damned right I will, but maybe I want *more* than a pardon. Maybe I don't want to go through the rest of my life with false charges of assault, rape, and manslaughter hanging over my head. Maybe I don't want a pardon as much as I want exoneration."

She looked quickly away. "You've got to get me out of here to get even the pardon," she reminded him. "You can worry about the exoneration later."

"The only way I'll ever get that is for you to tell the truth."

"You can go to hell! You'll get your pardon. That's enough!"

He nodded. "I suppose so. I'll get *my* pardon. But will *you?*"

"Who'd believe you instead of me, Kershaw?" she sneered.

He shrugged. "A hell of a lot of people who really know you, Milly."

Lee turned to study the terrain. It was as before. It was as deserted as a lunar landscape. "It was a long time after Queho and I were cellmates that he told me the truth about you and Ahvote," he said casually over his shoulder. "How you led the poor bastard on and let him take you in your quarters when your husband was out in the field and you had been hitting the bottle in private."

"My God! He told you *that?*" she exclaimed.

Lee looked steadily back at her. He shook his head. "No," he replied, "but *you* just did."

She had been neatly trapped. Her great blue eyes slid sideways toward the Winchester rifle.

Lee grinned. "You kill me, Milly, and you'll never get out of this country alive."

"Look," she said quickly. "I'll make it up to you, Kershaw. Do you want money? I can get it for you! I'll go to bed with you, if *that* is what you want. Ask me for *anything!* But for God's sake, don't say anything to Will about what you just said to me!"

He studied her for a little while. "God help you," he said quietly. "I don't believe anyone else can."

She had offered herself to this strange man and *he had turned her down!* Maybe he wouldn't talk about her when they got out of the *malpais* country, but for the rest of her life there would be the haunting fear that he *would* talk. She looked again at the rifle. The back of his head was only ten feet away from her—she could hardly miss at that range.

Lee heard the faint click of the rifle hammer as it was drawn back to full-cock. "The only person who can tell the truth about you, Milly, is yourself," he said without turning his head.

She let the hammer down to half-cock and stood up.

The heavy Sharps rifle flatted off and the inch-and-three-eights, 370-grain bullet explosively struck the breech of the Winchester. The woman screamed and involuntarily flung up her arms, letting go of the rifle. It arched out beyond the rocks with the moonlight shining on the fat-polished barrel to land on the steep, slick rock slope, and it slid and clattered down to come to rest fifty feet away from Lee, shining dully from the reflected moonlight.

Lee dragged the woman down into cover. A wisp of gunsmoke drifted off high on the slopes beyond the bulging cliff on the west side of the cave mouth above the talus slope. He looked back into the woman's drawn face. "Great," he said. "I ought to make you go down and get that rifle." She recoiled back from him. Lee turned away. "Milly," he politely suggested, "you ought to go back in the rocks and empty out your drawers. Keep your head down!"

The Sharps cracked again, and the exploding slug smashed the hammer from the Winchester. The breed must be using the Vollmer telescope. The third explosive slug smashed into the small of the stock and broke it.

Lee studied the slopes. The second and third shots had each come from a different position from the first shot. "Maybe four hundred yards," said Lee quietly. "The son-ofabitch could thread a needle with that damned Sharps."

Lee shaped a cigarette. As long as it was moonlight and he had no rifle, there was no chance of getting at the breed. Maybe Mildred was right—maybe they should get out of there while they could, but even so, they'd have to wait for darkness, and then the breed would have a chance to move in. Lee could make it through the darkness as silently as wind-driven smoke, but the woman was heavy on her feet, and Queho could hear like a hunting wolf.

"You're pressing your luck, Kershaw," the Nevada deputy had said.

Lee crouched low and lighted the cigarette. As he raised his head, a puff of smoke swirled upward. The Sharps exploded, this time nor more than three hundred yards from where Lee lay hidden. The slug exploded against a rock twenty feet behind Lee and in front of where Mildred was busy. There was no sound from the woman. She had learned enough not to reveal her presence by sight or sound.

Lee ground out the cigarette and replaced it by a cut of Wedding Cake. He worked up the sauce. The moon was sailing westward. Before long, the shadows would fall across the *malpais* country and fill in the canyon that led to the outside world.

Lee crayfished backward, low on his lean belly, head turned sideways and close against the harsh earth.

The Sharps was fired. This time it was not more than two hundred yards away. The slug exploded right where Lee had been hiding. He crayfished with greater speed back into the shelter of the rocks where Mildred lay hidden. Shadows crept across the *malpais*. Lee worked his way back deeper into the labyrinth, hoping to God he wouldn't arouse an unhappy rattlesnake that might have been flushed from its hole by the flash flood.

Lee reached far over and placed his hat on a rock. The

bullet drove through it from one side to the other, going in small and coming out big enough for Lee to put his fist through as it landed in front of him.

The moonlight now shone only on the cliff faces of the northeast, while the canyon to the west of them and the rock labyrinth southwest were shrouded in shadow darkness. Lee worked his way farther and farther into the labyrinth. He wrinkled his nose. He had caught Milly's scent, that is, the scent she had left behind her. "Milly?" he softly called. There was no reply. Lee risked standing up, then catfooted deeper and deeper into the labyrinth. Maybe she had gone to ground nearer the river heights. Twenty minutes later, he knew she had left altogether. He looked toward the darkened canyon. "Good luck," he said quietly.

A breeze sprang up. Metal clicked against rock high on the moonlit slopes overlooking the labyrinth, and Lee hit the ground a fraction of a second before the Sharps bellowed and sent an explosive bullet whispering right over where Lee had been standing. The bullet blew itself up against the rocks fifty yards beyond Lee. The breed sonofabitch was shooting by instinct. No living man could have seen Lee in those shadows—no living man other than Queho, that is.

TWENTY-SEVEN

"HAVE YOU KILLED him?" Lucille asked Queho.

Queho squatted behind a rock ledge, still bright in the now waning moonlight, priming his three cartridge cases. "How did he get the other woman?" he asked.

"She saw him from the cave and went to him," lied Lucille.

"So he didn't get into the cave?"

She shook her head. "The other woman followed him toward the river," she lied again. "He never saw the cave."

He looked at her with the moonlight on his dark face and with his strange, light eyes that seemed to glitter like running water. "Why you not go with woman? Why you come to me, eh?" he asked.

She could not look at his eyes. "To warn you, Queho," she replied.

"That Kershaw come to kill me?" He laughed.

"He was sent to get us women. He has taken two of them now."

Queho shrugged. "Maybe he'll quit when he is ahead."

She shook her head. "You know him better than that, Queho."

He measured 70 grams of powder into a cartridge case. "Why you warn me that he come?" he asked.

"I didn't want to see you get killed."

He wadded the case. "Or maybe Kershaw either?"

She nodded. "I don't want to see *anyone* get killed, Queho."

He shook his head. "One of us will have to die."

"Can't you let him go?"

"He knows now where Queho's cave is! The woman will tell him!"

"So do I! So do Amy and Mildred!"

"No difference. Them women couldn't find this place again and wouldn't come back to show the way even if they could."

"I can," she said.

He filled another cartridge case. "You're still here," he reminded her. His strange eyes slid sideways to look at her pale face. "You stay with Queho, eh? Why?"

She shook her head. "Look," she said quickly. "Let me go and talk with Lee Kershaw. Maybe he'll take you back alive for trial. If you let me go, there may be amnesty for you."

He filled the last of the three cases with the last of his powder. "What *that* mean?"

"They'll go easy on you because of what you did."

He threw back his head and laughed. "Women!" he said. "They believe only what they want to believe." He looked at her. "You know what they do to Queho? Kill on sight! Like mad dog! They cut off head and take back in a sack to prove they got me! You think I am a fool!"

"But maybe Lee Kershaw can help you!"

He placed the wads into the mouths of the two cartridges and pressed them into place. "No," he said firmly. "Kershaw not help me." He placed one of his three remaining bullets into the chamber of the rifle and seated it firmly into the barrel with the bullet-starter. He slid in a long cartridge case and raised the rifle breech. He looked beyond the place where they were hidden. "I kill Kershaw," he insisted. "After that, stay here in the *malpais* with plenty food, water, guns, and tobacco." He slanted his eyes at her. "Maybe with woman too?"

She did not answer him. He placed the long-barreled rifle on a flat rock and peered through the scope. There were deep shadows where Lee had last been hiding. If he knew Lee Kershaw, the man would come through the darkness to find Queho. "How many guns Kershaw have?" he asked over his shoulder.

"Why, two I think. A rifle and a pistol."

"You sure about that?"

"Yes." Then she remembered how Lee Kershaw had destroyed Queho's supplies and arsenal. "Simple strategy," he had said. "I'm destroying his arsenal and his base of supplies. I wish to God I could dry up the Colorado River so that he'd be out of water too."

Queho laughed. "He's only got a pistol *now.*" He patted the engraved breech of the Sharps rifle. "When daylight come, Kershaw dies. No chance for him. No chance at all."

"And the woman with him?"

He looked bact at her. "I have three rounds left," he replied.

"You don't want her anymore?"

"I never did," he replied. "Only wanted her to suffer and then die for what she did to me."

"And to Kershaw also?"

"I was thinking of myself," he said.

"And you want me?"

He did not look at her. The shadows were creeping up the long slope, erasing the bright moonlight.

"I asked you a question," she said.

"You want *me?*" he asked.

Lucille closed her eyes. "Only if you will give yourself up, Queho."

Long minutes ticked slowly past. "No deal," said Queho at last.

Stone clicked against stone in the deep quiet of the canyon. A shadow seemed to detach itself from a rock and move swiftly toward the next one. Queho fired at the movement. The smoke drifted down the slope, obscuring his vision. Mildred Felding lay flat behind the rock, breathing harshly, pressing her sweating face against the harsh earth. The gunshot echo died away down the canyon.

Queho snapped down the breech lever and the smoking cartridge case slid out. He seated the next to the last bullet and loaded the cartridge case in behind it. He closed the rifle breech and removed the Vollmer scope. He put the scope into its case and took the vernier tang sight from its little case. He fitted the sight into its mounts and screwed it home. "Scope no good at night," he said, almost as though to himself.

Queho looked at the girl. "You want to go?" he asked.

"You'll let me?"

"If you want," he replied. His eyes searched her face.

"I'll go only to talk with Kershaw."

"Waste of time," he said.

"If he won't agree to help you, I'll come back to you."

"Why?"

She hesitated. "Maybe because I want to."

"You know future? I'll tell you—heat, poor food, lousy water, loneliness. . . . Loneliness the worst. Man goes loco from that. Kill slowly. Maybe better to die by posse bullet than go like that. Maybe a year; maybe five years; maybe twenty. *¿Quien sabe?*"

"But, if I were with you, it would not be so."

He laughed. "You loco already from being here too long." His dark face changed. "You go now. Call out to Kershaw. Tell him you coming. If you want to come back, you come at dawn, so I can see you. No tricks, eh?"

She shook her head.

"Go now," he repeated. "Before I change mind."

"Kershaw!" she called clearly. "Lee Kershaw!"

"Kershaw . . . Lee Kershaw . . . ," echoed the canyon.

There was no reply.

Queho grinned. "Maybe he think I shoot by sound. Maybe he right." He laughed.

"Lee Kershaw!" called the girl. "I'm coming down!"

"Don't shoot, goddamn you, Kershaw!" yelled Queho. "You shoot girl and you shoot pardon all to hell!" He roared with laughter.

"Come on down!" called Lee. He moved as soon as he yelled.

Queho looked at the girl. She stood up and hesitated. The breed said nothing. Maybe that is what she had expected. She climbed over the rocks and vanished from sight.

Queho listened. He could hear her progress down the long slope into the deep shadows of the canyon. Then it was quiet again. The moon sank lower, and the shadows came up the slope and covered Queho and his rifle, but he was still there, listening, listening.

TWENTY-EIGHT

"YOU'LL HAVE TO get that rifle of his," insisted Lee.

She sat wearily in the darkness. She could hear Lee chewing the tough and stringy meat he had taken from the cave. "I can't do that," she repeated for the third time.

"I don't trust him," repeated Lee for the third time.

"He doesn't trust you!"

He shrugged. "You see? It's hopeless. I'm taking you out of here before dawn comes and lights up this canyon like a Fourth of July fireworks display. I've done what I came to do. I never agreed to do anything about Queho."

"I promised him I'd come back to him if you wouldn't agree to help him."

He shook his head. "No go. Let him sit up there without his arsenal and his food. He'll get smart when he needs water."

"What will happen to him?"

He shrugged again. *"¿Quien sabe?* He's wanted by Nevada, California, and Arizona." He looked sideways at her. "You know how much combined reward money has been offered for him? *Five thousand dollars!* I could use that money!"

"But you said you didn't want him!"

He nodded. "That's right. I can't risk trying to take him when I have to deliver you and Milly back to get my pardon."

"But will you help him?"

"He's beyond help."

She covered her eyes with her hands. "I'll have to go back to him then."

Lee stowed a wad of Wedding Cake into his mouth and worked up the rich sauce. After a while, he spat to one side. "Tell you what," he suggested. "You go back up there and get that damned rifle of his away from him, and I'll talk business with him. Personally, I think you're wasting your time."

The girl didn't rise to the bait right off.

Lee rested his back against a boulder. He did not look directly at the girl, as though what she agreed to do was really of no concern to him. She wasn't too bright.

"He won't give it up," she said.

"Possible," he agreed. He spat to one side.

"What if he does?" she asked.

Lee wiped his mouth with the back of a hand. "I'll feel a hell of a lot safer talking to him."

"You're not lying to me?"

Lee acted shocked. "Me? Lee Kershaw! I'm known far and wide as a man of my word."

"Can I believe that?"

He leaned forward. "Listen," he said tensely. "I gave my word to your uncle's secretary and to Colonel Felding that I would not try to escape, but that I would try to get you women back to safety. By this time I could have been safely in Mexico or Canada. Did I go? No! Doesn't that prove I keep my word?"

"And you'll give me your word that no harm will come to him if I get his rifle for you?"

Lee leaned back again. "I give you my word that no harm will come to him from me, if you get his rifle from him," he promised.

She sat there for a long time. Lee was dying for a smoke, but he knew if he lighted a cigarette that damned breed might put a bullet through his head.

"All right," she agreed at last.

"Call out to him then that you'll come up the slope at first light of dawn."

"And I can tell him that you'll help him?"

Lee nodded. "But don't tell him about the rifle."

"He won't let me get near it."

"You'll have to figure that one out."

"He won't leave it."

"Then goddammit, you've got to make him leave it!"

"But how?"

"Promise him the damned moon. Promise him anything!"

She nodded. "All right," she agreed. "If it will save his life, I'll promise him anything."

Lee shifted his chew and spat. He wiped his mouth. "You stay here then."

"Alone? Why?"

He grinned in the darkness. "Because if that damned breed comes through the darkness looking for me, he'll locate me by finding you, and *I* don't aim to be around in case he does come."

He was gone into the darkness.

TWENTY-NINE

THE FIRST PALE, pearl-gray light of the dawn flushed against the eastern sky. A cool wind swept through the canyon, ruffling the surfaces of the pooled rainwater.

"Queho!" called the girl.

"Queho . . . Queho . . . Queho . . . !" dutifully echoed the canyon.

There was no reply.

Lee lay well back watching the opposite slopes through Queho's powerful field glasses. Nothing moved.

"Queho!" called the girl.

"Queho . . . Queho . . . Queho . . . !" repeated the canyon.

Silence again.

Lucille glanced back over her shoulder. There was no sign of Lee Kershaw. Maybe he had left during the night.

Lucille walked across the floor of the canyon and paused at the foot of the slope. There was no sign of life. She looked back toward where she thought Kershaw must be hidden. There was no sign of life.

She started up the slope. Loose rock clattered and slid down the steep slope, awakening the canyon echoes.

Lee refocused the glasses. "Sonofabitch," he breathed. He could pick out the dark rodlike shape of the rifle barrel between two boulders. The barrel moved even as he looked, and he instinctively ducked his head. Slowly he raised his head. The rifle barrel was gone and the girl stood just this side of the boulders behind which Queho was hidden.

"I'm here, Queho!" she called out.

"Come on," he invited. He did not show himself.

She clambered over the boulders and sat down near him, breathing hard from her exertions.

"Well?" asked the breed.

"He's gone," she replied.

He narrowed his eyes. "You sure?"

She shrugged. "I couldn't find him."

"He's down there somewhere!"

"Maybe, but I didn't see him," she lied.

He nodded. "All right. We go back into cave. Get food. I need powder and bullets for cartridges."

She was desperate. Once he took her back into that cave, Lee Kershaw would have no chance of dealing with him. "It's no use," she said. "There's nothing in there anymore."

"What the hell you mean?" he demanded.

She shrank back from his fierce gaze.

"It was Kershaw," she explained. She told him what Kershaw had done in his cave.

"You mean everything gone?" he demanded. "Food, guns, powder, *everything?* Goddamn you! You lied to me! You say he not get to cave!"

She nodded. "I was afraid of what you might do if you knew about it!"

He looked back up the slope toward the hidden entrance to his hideout. "Jesus God!" he yelled. "I got to get bullets and powder!"

"It's all gone," she insisted.

Lee could hear the echoing voices but could not distinguish any words. He wished to God he had a rifle as he saw Queho's head pop up from behind the boulders. Then he saw the breed run up the steep slope toward the cliff face, *and he did not have his rifle with him.*

Lucille watched Queho vanish in among the rocks where the cave entrance was concealed.

"Now!" yelled Lee.

"Now . . . now . . . now . . . !" yelled the canyon.

She looked down at the long rifle and then up the slope. If he came back while she was taking the rifle to Lee. . . .

"Now! Goddammit!" shouted Lee. He jumped over a boulder and started to run down the slope.

She picked up the rifle.

"Get the cartridges and the gear!" yelled Lee.

She should have gotten wise then, but she did not. Dutifully she picked up the tools and parts and the two cartridge cases, one empty and the other loaded with the last of Queho's powder.

Lee sprinted across the canyon bottom, a clay pigeon if Queho changed his mind and returned from the cave.

The girl hesitated.

"You may save his life by bringing that rifle here!" yelled Lee.

She scrambled over the boulders. She ran down the slope. She tripped and fell and the rifle dropped to the ground. It spat flame and smoke and the slug whipped through the air a foot over Lee's head. He ran up the slope and grabbed the smoking rifle. He gripped the girl by an arm. "Hang onto the gear," he ordered her. He hustled her and the rifle down the slope and across the bottom of the canyon, expecting at any second to hear a gun report behind him and to feel the impact of one of Queho's pistol bullets.

He pushed her over the boulders. He let the rifle down beside her and looked back over his shoulder. The far slope was empty of life. He rolled over the boulders and landed on his hands and knees with his chest heaving and trembling and with the fresh sweat dripping from his bearded face. For a minute, he thought he was going to get sick.

The girl wiped the sweat from her face. She placed the tools and other items beside the rifle and looked down at them. "Why do you need those?" she slowly asked.

Lee opened the breech of the rifle and saw the spent cartridge case kick out from the impact of the strong ejector.

He caught the case and placed it on the ground. He opened the brass can of bullets and pushed the last one of them into the rifling ahead of the chamber by means of the bullet-starter. "Have you more bullets?" he asked.

"All you wanted was the rifle so that he couldn't use it against you," she said. "He's gone to his cave to get bullets and powder."

Lee took the last of the loaded cartridge-cases and slipped it into the chamber. He raised the breechblock by means of the lever. He shook the brass powder-box. It was empty. "One goddamned round," he softly cursed.

"That's why he went back to his cave," she repeated.

"And he trusted you with his beloved rifle, eh?" Lee grinned like a hunting lobo.

She stared at him. "What do you mean?" she asked suspiciously.

He raised the vernier tang sight and sighted through it toward the far side of the canyon. "Maybe eight hundred yards," he said thoughtfully to himself. "Better use the Vollmer scope."

"Kershaw!" she cried. "You gave me a promise!"

He removed the vernier tang sight and replaced it with the slim tube of the Vollmer scope, which was almost as long as the barrel itself. The sun was already beginning to strike the canyon and its slopes. The air was still sharp and clear. There was no heat haze and no shimmering of the atmosphere as yet. That would come with the greater heat of the day.

She reached out a trembling hand toward him. "Kershaw!" she pleaded.

He looked at her. "Shut up!" he ordered. "And keep your head down!"

He shaped and lighted a cigarette. He rested the long rifle on the flat-topped ledge directly in front of him and with his dirty right hand gripping the small of the stock. The cigarette smoke wreathed about his lean, bearded face in the shade of his low-pulled hatbrim. Patiently he waited.

"Kershaw," she said after a time.

He did not look back at her. "Yes?" he asked.

"You'll go to hell for this," she promised him.

He shook his head. He did not take his eyes off the sunlit slope far across the wide canyon. "I've already been there," he told her. "Remember, I was in Yuma Pen in the summer."

She was silent after that.

Patiently he waited.

THIRTY

QUEHO PADDED INTO the cave entrance. He turned a corner and lighted a match. There was a lantern in a wall niche. He lighted it and catfooted along the tunnel until he reached the end of it overlooking the deep natural pit. He hooked the lantern bail over his left arm and went quickly up the rope ladder. He reached the top and held out the lantern to survey his hideout. He cursed softly as he hurled the bedding to one side to hunt for anything Kershaw might have overlooked. It was no use.

He looked at his empty weapons-rack. He ripped open the ammunition box where he had kept his extra six-guns, only to find it empty. The extra rounds for the big Sharps .40/70 were all gone. His breathing was harsh and heavy. He padded to the rear of the cave and slipped his hand under a ledge to retrieve a bottle of forty rod. He drank deeply, his throat working convulsively.

He unsheathed his Colt and half-cocked it. He opened the loading gate and twirled the cylinder. He slipped a round into the one empty chamber and snapped shut the loading gate. He replaced the Colt in the holster. He drank again.

He walked to the mouth of the cave and looked down the long talus slope. He could see the entrance to the water tunnel, now completely blocked by the collapsing of the roof. The nearest secret access to the river was some miles upstream, and Kershaw might have someone watching it from the Arizona side of the river. Queho might reach water ten miles downstream, but it was too close to the outer world, and Nevada kept a posse working in that area. The collected rainwater in the *malpais* would be gone by the next day under the broiling heat of the summer sun.

Queho squatted in the cave, drinking steadily. The girl had told him that Kershaw had dumped all the disabled weapons, the food, ammunition, powder, and other gear down into the pit. *Enju!* He, Queho, would go down into the pit and see what he could salvage.

He drank again and thrust the half-empty bottle inside his shirt. He hooked the lantern bail over his left arm and reached down with his left hand to grip the ladder. The lantern slipped from his arm and dropped into the pit. He heard it crash far below. The glass cylinder shattered and the oil reservoir split itself against a rifle breech. The oil leaked out and was caught up by the hungry flames. An eerie dancing light showed far below.

Queho got onto the ladder and hung there looking down into the depths. He could just make out the disabled weapons and some of the boxes of food. He let himself slowly down the ladder and reached the tunnel. He leaned out and began to ripple-shake the ladder until the hooks at the top released themselves from the upper end of the heavy pegs he had driven into the rim of the pit. The upper end of the ladder fell down and past Queho to strike its heavy iron rungs against a can of Kepauno Giant blasting powder, splitting the can wide open, so that the loose powder poured over the leaping flames. The other powder cans at the bottom of the pit exploded like an erupting volcano, and the narrow shaft funneled the flames, smoke, gas, and debris up the shaft as though it was a gigantic shotgun barrel. The blast struck Queho on the face and upper body and hurled him backward into the tunnel, where he lay half stunned with the searing agony of the burned flesh still to come through the sudden numbness of great shock.

THIRTY-ONE

IT WAS THE rumbling roar from what seemed like a solid rock cliff face that aroused Lee. Smoke poured out from the hidden entrance to the cave and drifted slowly upward in the windless air. It was thick, so thick that it masked the cliff face, so that when Queho did appear, his appearance startled Lee as though the devil himself had been conjured up from the depths of hell.

Queho walked slowly downslope through the smoke and made no effort to conceal himself.

Lee picked up the powerful glasses and focused them on the breed. "For the love of God," he breathed. At that distance the breed seemed to have been painted black from the waist up.

"What is it?" asked Lucille.

Lee lowered the glasses. "He must have been hit by the explosion. Look for yourself."

She raised the glasses and focused them. She turned her head away, sickened at the sight. "I'll go to him," she said bravely.

Lee shook his head. "No. You can do him no good."

"I can take care of him," she insisted.

He looked back at her. "No," he repeated. "I'm taking you out of here."

"You're only thinking of yourself!" she cried. "You won't get your pardon and the reward money unless you kill him and bring me out! Is that it?"

"Partly," he agreed. He looked across the sunlit canyon

toward the breed who stood there, seemingly staring across the canyon with eyes that could not see and would never see again. "Look at him," he suggested to the girl. "He's all alone. No supplies. No weapon other than a six-gun. Those are third-degree burns or I miss my guess. He'll be in terrible agony within a short time. Even a doctor can't do much good for him now."

It was very quiet in the canyon. Queho did not move.

"What will you do?" she asked. "The decision is yours, Kershaw."

Lee passed a hand across his eyes. The words of Will Felding aboard the *Mohave* came back to him: "It seems to me that it would be much less expensive, plus the bother of bringing a man to trial after months of feeding and quartering him, then the wages of the manhunter, the guards, the other personnel involved, sir! How much easier to put a bullet into your quarry and report that he resisted arrest, eh, Kershaw?" Then Lee had made his brave reply: "That would make me judge, jury, and executioner, sir. I *hunt* men. I do not judge them, or *execute* them."

It was a long shot and there was but one bullet. If Lee missed, he might never get near enough to use the six-gun on the breed.

"It's like judging an animal with a broken leg," said the girl. "Let him go, Kershaw."

Lee shook his head.

"He can destroy himself if he must," she added.

He shook his head. "And wander in limbo forever, shunned by the other spirits of his people?"

"You speak of him now as though he was a full-blooded Mohave Apache," she said.

He looked at the breed and then back at the girl. "Now," he said quietly, "he *is* acting like a full-blooded Mohave Apache."

"Then there is no hope for him?"

"None," replied Lee.

She waited a little while as the sun warmed the canyon.

Lee did not look at her again. "Start walking down the canyon," he said. "You can't get lost. There is only the one way. I'll catch up with you in a little while. We will find Milly further along, most likely. She can't have gotten very far."

She was quiet for a while as she looked across the canyon at Queho. Then she turned on a heel and walked down the slope toward the bottom of the canyon. Soon, the sound of her footsteps vanished. A light morning breeze began to blow up the canyon.

Lee shaped and lighted a cigarette. He drew in on it several times, then threw it over the rocks to land on the slope. The slight wind drifted the thin spiral of smoke toward the south. Lee full-cocked the Sharps rifle and squeezed the rear trigger. The front trigger set with a tiny click. Lee placed the tip of his trigger finger flat on the front trigger. He drew in a deep breath as he sighted, allowing for the slight crosswind, across the sunny canyon toward the distant figure standing motionless on the sunlighted slope. He let out half of his breath, steadied his aim, and squeezed off the shot.

The girl heard the slamming sound of the big rifle as it was fired. The echo flatted back and forth between the canyon walls and died away. It was very quiet again. The girl did not look back.